The hesitant huntress . . .

"So you like emeralds?" the earl pressed, closing the distance between them.

"No. Yes. That is . . ." Andrea realized she was babbling. She should be intimidating *him,* not backing into the marble. *Pay no attention to how tall he is,* she warned herself. *Or how nicely built.*

But he was there, so near and overwhelming. And he was staring quite rudely at her lips.

Flustered, she blurted out the first thing to come into her head. "You cannot mean to kiss me?"

His lips curved into a grin. "And why not?"

The earl leaned closer yet, mere inches away. His voice was little more than a whisper, a caress of a sound so close to her ears. "My dear, any good flirt knows a kiss is not a declaration."

All she could see were lips, so firm and full, and so near above her. "N-no?"

"No indeed. It is a trifle, a thing of pleasure. It means nothing." His eyes focused on her mouth, which had gone suddenly dry. One inch more and they would touch. "Shall I show you?"

Catch Of The Season

Barbara Benedict

JOVE BOOKS, NEW YORK

CATCH OF THE SEASON

A Jove Book / published by arrangement with
the author

PRINTING HISTORY
Jove edition / January 1991

ISBN: 0-515-10471-X

Jove Books are published by The Berkley Publishing Group,
200 Madison Avenue, New York, New York 10016.
The name "JOVE" and the "J" logo
are trademarks belonging to Jove Publications, Inc.

To Maude and Paude,
This one's for you.

CHAPTER

1

"Guests!" roared Richard, the most recent Earl of Fairbright. "Arriving when?"

He stomped forward, failing to notice the mud he ground into the drawing room carpet. Nor did he heed that instead of faded gray, said rug was now a fresh, effeminate rose.

The cause of his anger sat upon a high-backed chair, perched like a queen on her throne, eyeing his approach with infuriating complacency. Resting her wrinkled, jewel-encrusted hands on a cane, his aunt, the dowager Lady Sarah, spared a tight, triumphant smile. "I daresay they will be prompt. Ain't a mother in England to balk at selling the family jewels to net you. Combine the Fairbright title with your dark good looks and occasional charm, boy, and you have no choice but to be the catch of the Season."

It was deuced insulting to be regarded as a fish, he thought. A prize one, to be certain, but strip away the title, the vast holdings and wealth, and all one had was a man. And at this moment, a distinctly unhappy one.

Looking away to regain his temper, Richard now noticed the changes in the room. Instead of silver stripes, the walls sported pink roses. The velvet drapes had vanished; dainty lace curtains flitted at the casement windows in their place. Indeed, all the decent furnishings were gone, replaced by some silly French things, the designer of which he neither knew nor cared about, in a clear case of his comfort being sacrificed to fashion.

His favorite chair had no doubt been the first to go. Lady Sarah was blind to how sturdy and comfortable it was; she saw only its erupting insides. Women had no conception of the importance of comfort, he fumed. Appearance was their sole priority.

This brought his gaze to the mantel. As expected, his father's portrait was gone. The ormolu clock had returned.

Blast the woman; was nothing sacred? She must be brought to accept that this was his house now. If she wanted another museum, she could revamp her own establishment in London. And she could take her gewgaws with her. He went for the clock, prepared to toss the gaudy thing through the nearest window, unmindful of the mud he left in his wake.

Lady Sarah, however, missed nothing. Her puckered features wrinkled moreso, especially the nose. "Remove those boots before you take one more step. Gads, Richard, I have seen stable boys finer garbed than you."

He paused to run a hand through his tangled brown hair, belatedly aware of the stains on his buckskin breeches. True, he could have tidied up a bit, but, dammit, he'd been hard at work. As was invariably the case, her dictatorial summons had goaded him into acting first and regretting it later.

His fingers tightened on the clock. "What is this doing here again? Where is my father's portrait?"

"Safe enough in your study." She sniffed. "I will have no reminders of Alan's perfidy."

He whirled to face her. Any perfidy, Richard firmly felt, lay at his uncle's door. It was he who had cut off Richard's father and then reached out from the grave with the little-known proviso that should Richard inherit the title, he must do so without the Duncan wealth.

Knowing his uncle for an embittered old miser, Richard could resign himself to this, but he'd expected more of his aunt. "Perfidy?" he repeated, long-standing loyalty pushing him to his father's defense. "All the poor man did was follow his heart. Reggie was the heir then; my father was free to wed where he wished."

"Duncans *do not* marry trade!" Rather than continue her lecture, she forced a smile. "Which reminds me. I have arranged for the proper raiment to be laid out. I suggest you retire to your room to bathe and change."

He didn't know which stunned him more: her gall, or the obscure manner in which she switched the subject. Both left him a trifle uneasy.

Leaving the clock, he approached her chair. "Exactly what lies in that devious brain of yours now?"

"Don't talk fustian. Of course you must be presentable to greet your guests."

"Do you never listen? I have no time for guests. Nor the staff to serve them. Have you forgotten Mrs. Bumfrey is abed with a bad back again? And Lord knows the rest are too dim-witted to do more than scrape together a meal."

"I have summoned my own staff from London. Until they arrive, Lot can butler."

"Reggie's valet?" In that case, Richard thought, they'd best lock up the family silver, for only criminal negligence would place a man of Lot's ilk in charge of a house. "I have inherited headaches enough from the rest of my cousin's inept staff without adding his havey-cavey manservant to them."

"Lot will do in a pinch," Lady Sarah snapped. "And before you run through a list of other excuses, I can assure you the house is in prime condition for entertaining. That, since you clearly failed to notice, is what I have been doing here the past month or so."

Busy with the estate, Richard had noted little more than the color of the pillow slip he fell upon late each night. If he thought about the recent bustle at all, he assumed it to be but another of the renovating jaunts of which she seemed so fond. He was inclined to condone such creative release, anything to make her visits easier, but this time she had gone too far. Rearranging his house was one thing; his life was quite another.

"I have no time," he told her again. "There is the milking, plowing, and fleecing to do. Tenant cottages to build. And I have yet to begin the repairs to Hazard Hall."

"That castle again?" She slammed down her cane dangerously close to his toes. "The place is in utter ruin. Another good storm and it will be swept to sea."

"Then too will a major portion of family heritage. The first earl sweat his blood for that ruin, madam. Duncans have lived and fought and died within its walls."

Richard wondered why he argued. He knew she wanted it restored as much as he. Unfortunately, she wanted it done by her son, not a usurping nephew. Reggie could have received more than ample funds for the task, had he shown the least interest. And had he not broken his neck in a drunken curricle race last May.

"Without its castle," he persisted nonetheless, "Fairbright would be but another manor. As indistinguishable as the many females you forever contrive for me to meet."

"Ah, but these girls are most distinguishable." She then purred, with a most unsettling gleam in her eye, "Indeed, we have assembled the very cream of the ton."

"We?"

"Stop scowling; your eyes are dark enough as it is. If you must know, Violet and Amelia agree that if you are too busy to go to town, we must simply bring London here to you."

The Tribunal? There would be no stopping this if that trio of old crones joined forces. "Splendid. And just how much of the ton have you three assembled?"

"Enough for the competition."

"Compe . . ." He swallowed, then tried again. "What is it to be, an auction? I am no longer to be a fish, but rather a prime piece offered by Tattersalls?"

"Don't be vulgar. We have merely arranged a hunt of sorts. Your guests shall answer questions about Fairbright history in their quest for the prize. A clever diversion, don't you agree? After all, we must keep the twenty competitors, not to mention their mamas and chaperons, from each other's throats for the fortnight they will be here."

"A fortnight? Madam, this time you have exceeded eccentricity. If you think I can or even *will* play the congenial host for two weeks, you've gone stark staring mad."

She sat placidly, prepared to let him vent his rage without yielding an inch.

"I see what you mean to do," he said. "Parading these women before me, hoping I'll fall in love with one of them."

"Love has nothing to do with it!" The cane hovered again before settling tamely on the floor. "This estate must have an heir, boy. I will not have it pass to a stranger. And when one considers Horatio, I daresay a stranger man has yet to be born."

That hit home. His cousin Horatio was not only missing a screw or two, but the man seemed to have the Midas touch in reverse. The thought of leaving the manor in such inept hands stopped Richard cold.

Yet if his aunt sensed his hesitation, she'd merely use it to her advantage. "I know better than to involve myself with one of your schemes," he told her stiffly. "So kindly take your servants, *and* guests, and leave me alone."

"Gaining the title has turned you into a positive stick, boy. As a rake, at least you knew how to smile. Gads, go enjoy yourself for a change, or that scowl will become a permanent fixture. I can oversee the estate."

"God forbid!"

She raised a brow. "Such language proves a need for feminine influence. Not to mention the matrimonial pleasures. Something must be done about that scowl."

Useless, to engage in a verbal duel with her. Even at so advanced an age, her mind worked like a whip: quick, sharp, and punishing. "This is insane," he blustered. "One doesn't go about choosing a wife in so frivolous a fashion."

"You refused to select one in the more conventional manners. At nine and twenty, do you still not grasp what it means to be the earl? To do your duty? Fie, I should have known not to expect more."

Being the earl meant virtual poverty, Richard sneered. As his aunt well knew, for the bulk of the Duncan fortune had been left in her hands. Until her death, or unexpected generosity, Richard must slave dawn to dusk over the estate, fighting to reverse the ruin Reggie's gambling had brought to it. How could he take a bride when he was already wed to the land?

"My dear boy, must we bicker so?" As if suddenly deciding his vexation was contrary to her own best interest, his aunt tried a most unconvincing smile. "Let us instead strike a bargain. Humor me for a mere two weeks, playing the game by its rules—"

"Rules?" He raised a wary brow.

The cane fluttered harmlessly through the air. "Nothing to concern you. Simply follow them, and I will never again hound you about an heir."

"How tempting." Arms wrapped at his chest, he felt like a child clinging to his belligerency. Nonetheless, he shook his head. "But the fact remains, I have work to do."

"And what if I am prepared to pay for your time? Play my game, Richard, and you shall have all the funds you need to restore your castle."

He did not like the sudden leap his heart made. Do not trust her, he tried to warn himself, but he saw only the castle, as tall and proud as it was meant to be. "As much as I need?" he found himself asking. "You give your word?"

"The word of a Fairbright."

Her tone was as solemn as the words. Breaking such an oath was unthinkable, yet he could not bring himself to trust her. "I need merely play your game? Nothing else?"

"Skeptic. Let's just say I believe this game will net a bride." She simpered up at him. On a younger woman, such behavior might be called batting one's lashes, but the effect was more an owlish blink. "Indeed, I am prepared to wager half my fortune you shall find one amongst our guests to wed."

"Do not waste your money. I am done with all that."

"Because of Elysse Farrington? Bah, you cannot rue the shabby way that tart handled you the rest of your life. Count yourself fortunate she chose Parsett's title instead. Led the poor man on a merry dance, everyone says, before he took refuge in the grave."

He had no wish too discuss Elysse with anyone, least of all his I-told-you-so aunt. "And you, madam, have danced rather neatly around my question. What is your underlying motive? We both know you always have one."

With a sigh, she flashed a reluctant smile. "Never could gammon you. Very well, there has been talk in town. Your friends cannot see how a wild buck settled so readily into a bore. I cannot have it said I forced my nephew to toil his youth away."

She felt driven to still the gossips. He should have known.

"So I have included Foxley, Bellington, and Lennox in the hunt. For a mere two weeks, I hope you can prove to your friends you still know how to have a good time."

Richard had to admit he could enjoy a short respite— at the end of which he could begin fulfilling his father's dream of restoring the castle. "I suppose if I must." He leaned down, settling an elbow on the arm of her chair. "Let's strike a bargain then. I'll play your game, but only if that clock goes. I want my father's portrait where it belongs."

Her eyes narrowed. For a moment, he thought he had her, that she might refuse. Once again, he should have known better.

"Very well, if you give it a full two weeks. Adhere to all the rules, boy, and I will keep my end of the bargain.

Recklessly, he placed a hand on his chest. "The word of Fairbright."

"Splendid!" She had never worn a smile so generous. "Then I suggest you go up at once to prepare yourself. Your guests will be arriving momentarily."

"Momentarily?"

"Close your mouth, Richard. Gaping is most unattractive."

"Can't have that," he scowled. "Wouldn't want our giggling girls and their eager mamas taking it into their heads to leave."

"You can let that hope die, my boy. Every one of the chits is as deeply committed to this as you."

"Committed?" His irritation evaporated; the uneasiness returned. "To a silly game?"

"Ah, but it is so much more. They sacrifice the end of their Season."

"How much more," he pressed. Leaning closer yet, as he sensed a motive lying under her underlying motive.

"What did you offer that they would willingly take such a risk?"

"Cynic. Perhaps one or two are eager to learn more about Fairbright history."

"And I am the king of Egypt. Stop playing me for a fool, madam. I will know what you offered."

"I imagine they hope to net the prize."

"And what is the prize?" He straightened, understanding too late.

Triumph glittered in her smile as the cane banged down on his foot. "Why, *you,* of course!"

CHAPTER
2

God save the world from headstrong women, Richard raged as he stomped up the hill. What nerve his aunt had, thinking she could manipulate him. As if he would step so tamely into her trap. Catch of the Season, indeed. He was not a bloody fish!

An unfortunate comparison. His gaze went to the sea. Though he might not see the cove from here, Richard knew far too well the site of his ancestral home. He wished to be on the island now, gazing up at the ruins of Hazard Hall.

All the funds he'd need, his aunt had tempted. Heaven help him, how was he to resist?

Running an angry hand through his hair, he sat with a huff. It was a foolish thing, this obsession, for it made him vulnerable to his aunt's wiles. Her will. Still, it remained the sole legacy his father could leave him.

Too well he remembered that last day they'd spent together. Five he'd been at the time, scrambling to keep pace with Alan's longer legs as they walked along the beach, but he'd hungrily absorbed every word. History breathed in the huge tower, his father had explained. Generations of Duncans spilled their blood to preserve it for their sons, be they earl or younger brother, passing down the fruits of their lives with unending courage. A perseverance to take pride in, to pass down, from Duncan father to Duncan son.

As he did now, Alan had added solemnly, to his own child. Together they must promise to restore Hazard Hall, as a testimonial to all that bravery and endurance.

When his father died soon after, Richard had grasped those words to heart. There was no hope of the title then, not with his uncle and cousin in line before him, yet he was no less a Duncan. Perhaps more, for even at that age, he was deeply committed to the estate. Six years old he'd been, and as lean as a rail, but he would gladly have battled a hundred dragons to claim this land as his own.

Yet now, years later, with the battle ostensibly won, he seemed doomed to wrestle with twenty more. He frowned at the collection of dragons his aunt had assembled in the drive below. Carriage upon carriage had stalled there, spewing out gaggles of females shrieking and shoving one another aside in their haste to be admitted first.

Defiance flared anew. He must marry to provide an heir, he tried to accept that, but where in that stampede of feminine greed could he find anyone worth the sacrifice? Two weeks his aunt had committed to this game of hers. And Lord knew how many more would be spent dealing with the chaos left in its wake.

Marriage. Wincing, he pictured the bride she'd choose, one of those hothouse flowers London invariably bred, with a yard-long list of whims and a pout for every occasion. No, he insisted. He would wait for a woman he could love.

Yet, he had given his word. The word of a Fairbright, which was as binding as blood and far more solid than an outdated notion. Love was a luxury for poets and fools, something for which he could not afford to wait. Not unless he wished the dreaded Horatio as his heir.

A fine mess, he thought as he rose to his feet. Brushing his legs, he was hard put to decide which was more muddied: his life or his breeches. Perhaps his aunt was right and it was time to start changing them both.

"Oh, my. Forgive me. I had no idea anyone was here."

Soft and musical, the voice quivered across the air. As if physically touched, Richard whirled to face it. Shading his eyes with his hands, he discerned a slight form in the nearby copse, as colorless as the shadows around her. A governess, he thought with an odd stab of disappointment. Or someone's maiden aunt.

"Please forgive the intrusion, but I fear I am incurably inquisitive. I needed a peek at Fairbright Manor, you see."

Humility might color her words, but her pose spoke otherwise. Another headstrong woman, he revised. No doubt a sight-seeker, determined to meet the earl. He wondered how to get rid of her.

She stepped out of the shadows, extending a hand as firmly as any gentleman might. "I beg your indulgence for disrupting your solitude, Mr. er . . ."

Staring at the work-worn hand as it approached, Richard decided she must be a shop girl. Or perhaps the butcher's daughter. Were she to learn she had cornered the Earl of Fairbright, she'd never let him escape. "Uh, Richard," he said to deflect her. "Just call me Richard."

"And I am Andrea Morton." As he took the hand—it would have been rude not to—he was surprised by the warmth in that gentle grasp.

It forced him to notice other things as well. Though draped in black—and dust—and drab beyond belief, she flashed a smile that gave him pause. And those eyes. A vivid blue, they probed into him, so intently, he could feel their sting long after he looked away. "I, uh, am pleased to make your acquaintance, Miss Morton."

"Actually, it is *Mrs.* Morton."

"I see." There was a second equally unexpected stab. "Will Mr. Morton be joining us?"

"There is no . . . I mean . . . I am widowed."

Not pausing to analyze his relief, he caught a whiff of a sweet, floral scent. Tiny wisps of honey-brown hair escaped from the drab bonnet, making him wonder what might lie underneath. Giving rein to his imagination, he was aroused by the vision of a mass of golden-brown curls tumbling wild and free down her shapely back.

"My heavens. It certainly is huge, isn't it?"

As he realized she meant the view, he forced his thoughts back to self-preservation. Where they belonged.

"Uh, yes, though Barclay Hall to the south is far larger. But the Manor," he couldn't stop himself from ending proudly, "has been a Duncan stronghold for hundreds of years."

"Hundreds?" she muttered, as if impressed despite every attempt otherwise. "No wonder the earl is so arrogant."

"Arrogant?" Stung, Richard shook his head. "Proud, perhaps, but who wouldn't be, owning all this? Every stone in that house came from the land, madam. Each beam in the forty rooms of the central section came from the estate's forests. As did those in the outlying wings."

She shook her head with a sigh. "What a comfort it must be, knowing you can pass this on, generation to generation." She paused, then added under her breath, "If you're a man."

He ignored that, for he was launched. "Few homes can compare with its comfort and beauty. It has five separate gardens. The parkland even sports a maze. And those meadows stretching into the distance hold pastures and farmlands rivaled by none in all of England."

"You sound rather proud yourself. Do you work there?"

A logical conclusion, for all it rankled, yet he could hardly admit to being the earl now. "In a manner of speaking. My main concern is out at sea. See that winding road? Past the village and down the cliffs you will find a jetty. Once, it connected the small island to the mainland. Now, one must row across the cove to reach the castle I soon will, er, help restore there."

"I adore castles. How I would love to see it."

Not a tourist at all but a treasure-seeker? Richard bristled. Ever since Reggie had made public his absurdly desperate claim that the legendary Duncan doubloons lay hidden somewhere within the castle, every Tom, Jack, and Mary had been crashing the manor to try his luck.

"Perhaps someday," he temporized. "But I am curious, Mrs. Morton. What brings you to the neighborhood?"

"The earl. I am told he seeks a wife."

This was going from bad to worse. How bald those words seemed. And how chilled they made him feel. "I see. So you've come to watch the auction?"

She surprised him by giggling. "Isn't it just? Truly, it seemed more like Tattersalls than a sedate country party. One wonders how a man of his stature can subject himself to it. Though considering the rumors about town, I suppose he can subject himself to most anything."

The chill went to an absolute freeze. "Rumors?"

She seemed suddenly interested in his boots. "They . . . that is, I heard . . . without truly meaning to, of course . . . that his lordship spirited not one but three different cypri . . . er, ineligible females into Haversham Hall. They say Lady Violet went as purple as her turban."

"We all make mistakes in our youth. A man cannot spend the rest of his life atoning for them."

"Mistakes?" She giggled again. "Is that what they call his infamous midnight romp through Vauxhall Gardens?"

He could murder whoever had been flapping his lips. "His mistake there lay in trusting his friends. He was sleeping, you should know, when they took his clothes."

"Sleeping? In his cups, you mean. Every bit as foxed as he was for Bottomly's challenge, after being caught in, er, with the man's wife."

"You mistake him with another. Adultery is not at all in his line." Bad enough to hear his own sins enumerated, Richard thought; he did not intend to take on Reggie's as well. "Fairbright is quite miserably settled down now, I assure you. I've heard his aunt calls him a positive stick. As such, I daresay, he shall make a most superior husband."

"I suppose." She gave a rueful smile. "But such a boring one."

"Boredom, my dear woman, is matrimony's aim."

"However can you say so? It seems to me a man has everything his way. He can keep his gaming, his drinking, and, all too often, a mistress in every pocket."

Richard bristled. Though there might be truth in her words, a properly reared female should not discuss, nor even know about, such things.

"And yet," she nonetheless kept on, "unless a woman has money of her own, a staid and proper marriage is not only her inescapable fate but likely her only means of survival."

"I wonder which was Mr. Morton then," he countered. "A stick? Or a man with inordinately large pockets?"

"Neither." Proud and unrepenting, she faced him. "Mr. Morton was a pauper. And let me tell you, sir, being a woman in this world is hard enough; being poor on top of it forces hardships no man can ever know."

"Hardships," he mocked, irked into bringing her down a peg or two. "How dire you make it sound."

"Clearly, you have never endured a Season in London. Try being plucked and preened and dangled like headless fowl before the ogling buyers. The 'Marriage Mart' is all well and good if you're plumped in the pocket, but not when you are pinched, financially *and* bodily, and still they pass you by. After four long years of it, I think I was relieved to learn there wouldn't be funds enough for another."

"Four years, did you say?"

Hands clasped at her wrist, she looked down to the house with a determined gleam. "So you see, Fairbright is my final hope. I do believe I could cheat if it meant netting him."

When he didn't speak—shock erased his ability—she seemed to sense she'd gone too far. She turned, eyes soft and pleading. "Please forget I said that. It's just, well, I've worked so long and single-mindedly for this."

Richard refused to melt. "What of your poor host? Have you considered he might not enjoy being netted?"

"Oh, he will not mind." She drew in a breath, head held high. "Not once he sees what he gains in return."

Embarrassed for her, he looked away. When had she last glanced in a mirror? He thought of how his town-polished friends would laugh at such misplaced confidence. The scorn they would show for those ghastly, outmoded clothes.

Unfortunately, it wasn't their reaction that mattered but his own, and he did not like the way it softened now. Nor the way he kept remembering his own youthful bravado. Growing up here, he had often felt a similar stiff pride.

"The odds are against you," he snapped. "You have but one chance in twenty."

She beamed at the carriages in the drive. "Not at all. I have twice the chance of anyone else."

Too well he could picture her, using puny elbows to thrust to the front of the crowd. In all, he rather relished the shock she would feel to find himself there, transformed into the "arrogant," and unforgiving, Fairbright.

Perhaps she saw this in his face, for she turned a sudden pink. "I had best go. They will wonder what has become of me."

Richard said nothing. He would rather let the little baggage squirm.

"I—I had not meant to keep you in any case, Mr.—er—Richard. I am certain you have your own duties to perform."

"I do. Indeed, should I not report at once, there will be the very devil to pay."

"Truly?" The blue eyes went wide with dismay. "But it would be my fault. You must tell them I am to blame."

Thinking of his aunt's reaction to that, Richard smiled. "I doubt the dowager will listen."

"But this is terrible. I cannot allow you to suffer. I shall go down this very moment and tell Lady Sarah myself I am at fault. That I insisted you show me the estate."

So she meant to take him under her wing? Amused, and touched in spite of himself, Richard broadened his smile. "Thank you for the offer, but I hope it won't be necessary."

"So do I." Her own smile was quick, and swiftly withdrawn. "To be truthful, the woman terrifies me."

So she had met his aunt? That would mean the reverse was true. What, Richard wondered again, could prompt the old tyrant to invite such an unsuitable female? But perhaps Mrs. Morton was not alone. It would be so like his aunt to import a legion of gape-seeds, all to make the horse-faced Miriam Dennison, her perennial favorite, look good.

But perhaps his aunt would squirm a bit, if he

pretended to favor this Mrs. Morton. "Her bark is the worst of her," he said. "Face my aunt down, and she rarely bites at all."

"I shall try to remember that. And I do hope you will forget how I rattled on. Particularly the part about cheating. I can imagine how Lady Sarah might bark at that."

A poor choice of words on her part, but a timely reminder for his. His outrage revived, Richard saw only a pushy female manipulating him with her coy smiles.

Unaware of his change in mood, she continued, "I could wish for a chance to prove I am not normally such an addle-pate, though. Do you suppose we shall meet again?"

"I daresay we shall see quite a bit of each other." He gave a stiff bow. "Considering the circumstances."

He left her to make of that what she would as he hurried down the hill. Picturing her face when she learned he was the earl, he found he couldn't wait to change his clothes. So she thought he wouldn't mind being gammoned, did she? Cheating, for heaven's sake.

It was not until he had climbed the back stairs to enter his rooms that his mind made the inevitable leap. Pausing in the midst of tying his cravat, he grinned. Interesting concept, this cheating. Not that he'd stoop to anything as ungentlemanly as out-and-out fraud, but he could see nothing wrong in seeking an avenue for his own escape.

He paused, the grin now a frown. He had only a glimmer of an idea—hard to pin down—but something to do with this Mrs. Morton. There must be some way to use her to thwart his aunt. Only fair, considering how she meant to use him.

All at once, he felt a vast impatience to talk to her, to learn more about her past. Ah yes, they'd soon see who could outgammon whom.

• • •

In a room overlooking the drive, Lady Sarah motioned her two friends to join her at the window. Violet was looking pasty again, she thought. Though this, possibly, was due to the ridiculous purple she wore, donned for the sole purpose of eliciting sympathy. Give Lady Haversham an ear for a moment, and one could listen to her list of ailments into the night.

Amelia, on the other hand, was draped in disapproval today, looking like a puffed-up hen at her most belligerent. "I don't think we are being fair to the boy," she whined.

Already taxed by the day's events, Lady Sarah leaned heavily on her cane. "It is time my nephew found a bride."

"But look at them, Sarah. Screeching and carrying on. Is that what we want for our boy?"

Our boy, or our earl? thought Lady Sarah. Like the females in the drive below, Amelia had never once noticed Richard when Reggie was alive. It was the title that brought them all flocking to his side.

"Miffed about the lack of servants, I wouldn't doubt," she remarked aloud. "Let's watch them. Adversity tends to bring out the best and the worst in one."

Violet snapped her head around. "This is a test?"

"Sarah, you schemer." In her appreciation, Amelia moved closer to the window, her sulk forgotten. "You deliberately delayed your staff's arrival. What other tests have you in store for the poor chits?"

Lady Sarah gave a thin smile. "Enough to reveal who is best fitted to become the Fairbright bride."

"Good. We must have only the best for our Richard."

Violet sniffed into a lavender handkerchief. "But what if the wrong chit wins? Like Markton's widow, for example. I'd hate to see him tied to that Elysse Farrington person."

Sarah bristled. "My plan is foolproof. Only the perfect

mate for Richard can win. All we need do now is select a name. Remember, we must make our wagers tonight."

"Lady Elysse is formidably determined. I hear she has gone through most of Markton's money already."

"Ah, but do not forget Miriam. Or rather her mother. Agatha Dennison is a bulldog where her daughters are concerned. Unloaded three already on the unsuspecting ton."

"Perhaps, but they had looks to go with Dennison's money. Poor Miriam, on the other hand—"

"Girls, be still. Your wagers are to be kept secret and not divulged until the game is done."

"Sarah, darling, how diverting you are." Amelia's pique was a thing of the past, her love for gambling superseding any claims of conscience.

"Then I suggest you pay attention." Lady Sarah gestured to the sudden commotion in the drive below. Her smile broadened, and she placed less weight on the cane. "I do believe the hunt is about to begin."

CHAPTER

3

Eyeing the crowd bustling about the carriages in the drive, Andrea Gratham nearly lost heart. There were so many beautiful girls, she thought, and all so elaborately dressed. With a painful gulp, she felt the first stirring of doubt.

There was no comfort to be found in the house now. It loomed over her, cold and intimidating. *Intruder,* each gray stone seemed to accuse. *Fraud,* whispered the aging beams.

Her sister Cassandra would tell her to ignore such nonsense. Miranda would flounce her skirts and walk away undaunted, and Candida would never even notice. But then, those three sisters were quite confidently settled into their niches in life, while Andy herself . . .

"Enough of that," she said sternly. Continue in this vein, and she'd be spinning impossible dreams about the handsome man she'd just met. And that would never, ever do.

It had nothing to do with his being a common laborer. Indeed, that merely made him more attractive in her eyes, for she'd been fed to the eyebrows with preening fops and spineless aristocrats. Detesting snuff, French cologne, and all the rest of Society's affectations, she thought the man a nine days' wonder for having shirt points that not only failed to touch his ears but were frayed to near nonexistence.

No, she was not such a snob, for all that the Grathams could compare their line to any in the ton. The sad truth was that her wastrel father had gambled them into such a hole, she failed to see how anyone in the kingdom could be beneath her. Certainly not such a strong, appealing man.

She blushed, something she did not ordinarily permit herself to do. One single smile he had given her. However brilliant and devastating it might have been, it hardly lent itself to dreams. If the man thought of her at all, he could only consider her a total lackwit. In all that babbling, she had never explained the truth of why she was here.

Nor could she have. Her promise must come first. As always when her resolve wavered, she forced herself to remember her mother's wan, pinched face. She could be the sixteen-year-old Andy again, feeling the iron grip on her wrist. *Take care of your sisters,* the poor woman had pleaded. *See that they are cared for, that they marry well, for if left to your father, they will die unwed.*

It was an awesome promise for a child to make, and an even more difficult one to keep. Had she known then what it would entail, Andy might have argued a bit, but she had given her word to grant her mother peace. And thus committed, she had tackled the job full sail, knowing nothing was ever accomplished through whining.

Like the military strategist her father had been before drink got the best of him, Andy planned her campaign with care. Money was the cornerstone, and as her mother had warned, their father was too busy spending it to offer any. Forced to pinch pennies on the household accounts, Andy had no qualms over sneaking the occasional guinea from his pocket as Gerry Gratham dozed off a stupor on his rare visits home.

Yet when her sisters blossomed, and her funds did not, Andy graduated to pawning family treasures. With the coins safely stashed, she bullied their one remaining servant, Bess Jenkins, to teach her to sew. She practiced on threadbare linens, old draperies—whatever materials she could lay her determined hands upon—until she could copy any fashion plate from London. *Five wardrobes,* she'd recite as she wrangled for the muslins, cambrics, and silks that would mean her sisters' futures. *Five marriages to arrange,* she'd moan as she stitched long into the night.

But the difficulties mounted faster than the coins. As Gerry had alienated their few remaining relatives, Andy's search for a sponsor yielded little. Desperate, she resorted to their mother's cousin, Terese Dumont. Selfish to the bone, Terese conceded that while she might be duty-bound to sponsor her cousins' debuts, she would not take on the boring task of being their duenna.

So the nineteen-year-old Andy had garbed herself in unyielding black, curtailing a boisterous nature and any hope of finding a husband for herself, to become a prim and proper widow. As too few knew that Gerry even had daughters, who was to say the fictitious Captain Morton did not die in the Peninsular wars, leaving a young, penniless wife the only available chaperon?

When Candida turned seventeen, Andy's creations were lovingly packed between layers of tissue and carted off to London. All but three returned a few weeks later when Candida, bless her decisive heart, found and wed her curate.

After untold hours of alterations and worry, the lot was packed the following year for Miranda's Season. Six gowns were all Randy needed to find her dashing

dragoon. It left Terese to remark rather acidly that the
Grathams were not worth the bother of opening her town
house.

To disprove this, Cassandra prolonged her search a
full two years, using up gowns faster than Andy could
sew them. Still, she'd nabbed a peer—the answer to
Andy's prayers, had the pair not taken it into their heads
to elope. Disowned by his family, Cassandra's marquis
had less than a feather for them to fly with, but since all
three sisters were deliriously in love and as happy as
their mother could wish them, Andy forced a smile and
turned her sights on the twins.

The day they came of age, she went to her cache,
finding both funds and wardrobe dangerously depleted.
An inventory of the house yielded naught but her
mother's pearls to pawn, pearls the twins would need for
their debut. Cursing their father's neglect, enraged at her
helplessness, Andy paced the floor. The selfish cad had
wasted enough money on self-amusement, she decided.
It was time he faced responsibility. And she would
gleefully make him do it.

He must have known she was coming, for not six
hours prior, the drunken sot had flung himself from a
horse to his death. Anything to avoid obligation, she
later ranted at the solicitor. For all Gerry Gratham had
left behind were a mountain of debts, an estate entailed
to another, and the insurmountable doubt over what in
the name of Divine Providence his daughters were to do
now.

An appeal to their cousin was a waste of pride. Terese
had also spoken to the solicitor. As a veteran of too many
Seasons, she knew better than to bank on a pretty face,
not after having thrice been disappointed by the Gratham
girls. Instead, the wretch chose to spend the Season
touring the continent with her current paramour. The
girls could use her town house, Terese acceded, provided

they paid rent, in advance, and were gone before she returned.

Andy might smile to reassure the twins, but inside, her heart froze with despair. With no sponsor, no money, and a Season diminished by mourning, they had no hope. She began to suspect Divine Providence chose not to notice her at all.

This changed the lucky day she went to Hookham's Library. She had been half reading, half listening to the gossip about Fairbright's antics when the titters began about the upcoming *hunt*. Everyone who was anyone, it was said, planned to apply. Lady Sarah might be eccentric beyond permission, but the earl, by dint of his wealth and status, placed this latest scheme above reproach. Haste being her only advantage, Andy left both book and titterers where they were to speed home to her cousin's wardrobe.

Hands sliding over the rich materials, poor Andy nearly lost herself in that closet. She pictured herself in such gay confections, dancing and laughing and being admired. Andrea Gratham, Belle of the Ball. Or in this case, the Hunt.

But reality had reared its persistent head. The twins could not possibly attend without a chaperon. With Candy increasing, Randy on the continent, and Cassandra God-alone-knew-where, the dubious honor once again fell to her. Using her iron will, she had passed over the muslins and silks to settle on her own black cotton.

Once again the invisible widow, Andy went to the interview with Lady Sarah. If the dowager showed a marked lack of curiosity beyond the Gratham name, it did not signify. What did was that Andy emerged from the interview with an invitation. She carried it home on wings.

She returned to the wardrobe. It was not theft, she insisted as she snipped and altered the sophisticated styles to suit a debutante's needs. She meant only to appropriate, to make the girls presentable and convincing. If she took nothing for herself, surely Divine Providence would continue to guide them. Once her gamble paid off, she could replace the lot before Terese suspected a thing.

Good in theory, but now, facing the Manor, she realized euphoria had blinded her. Splendid wardrobe or no, she and her sisters did not belong here. There must be centuries of Fairbright ghosts, she thought with a gulp, lurking in every corner, condemning them as the frauds they were.

Nor could she hope the living would be less censorious. Not from what she had glimpsed of Lady Sarah. One word from any knowledgeable party and the dowager must surely demand they leave. One could hope the earl would defy her, but from what little she'd gleaned from the gossipmongers at Hookham's, such an act would require more backbone than this Reginald Duncan seemed to own.

"Andy, there you are. We thought we had lost you."

Her doubt dissolved at the sight of her sister's Dresden features. What man, with or without a spine, could resist those golden curls, such petal-soft skin, that angelic smile? As far as Andy could see, the only choice left to Fairbright was which twin he wanted more: the sweet-tempered Amanda or the more lively Pandora.

"M, where is P?" They had decided long ago upon using initials, feeling they could not possibly go about as Andy, Mandy, and Pandy.

"She was here a moment ago." Bess Jenkins, pressed into service as the necessary abigail, placed both hands on her ample hips as she scanned the milling crowd. "Botheration, now I've lost her too."

Andy tried not to groan. P could be anywhere in this mob. Considering the apparent ineptitude of Fairbright's staff, it could take hours to clear away the confusion of luggage and unsettled guests. And confusion, she knew, was a perfect breeding ground for Pandora's mischief.

"Likely bake in this heat, she will, and the blame will be on his lordship's head." The freshly starched cap and functional gray dress might proclaim Bess a meek lady's maid, but her tone and stance betrayed otherwise. She had watched over these girls from the cradle, she would boast to anyone, a task she planned to continue to her grave. "Never would see such hurly-burly at the Grange when my lady was alive, I can tell you."

Though there had never been guests at their home at all, Andy's innate sense of organization was likewise offended. "What host would invite so many females," she wondered aloud, "and then proceed to inconvenience them so? Where the devil is Fairbright, anyway?"

"Mind your tongue, miss. Remember, *devil* ain't a proper word for a lady to use."

While Bess was right, it did nothing for Andy's waning patience. "I shall be a pattern card of respectability if someone will just tell me which of these toplofty dandies is Fairbright. Is he the one in the beaver hat?"

"Oh, no! His name is Lord Foxley, and he's not the least toplofty. H-he helped retrieve my bonnet. When it blew off." The sudden color, as well as the prolonged sigh, told Andy her sister had less interest in Fairbright than she did. M had pinned her dreams on the puppyish good looks of this young nobleman and, hopeless romantic that she was, would be the very devil to dissuade.

There, she had used the word *devil* again and annoyed herself more in the process. "What about him?" She nodded at the next visible candidate.

M giggled. "I should hope not. That, P has learned, is James Bellington. A dyed-in-the-wool rake, from all reports, but she thinks him the outside of everything."

That he might well be, but the cad knew it. This was evident not so much in his looks, which were considerable, but more in the casual way he held himself. Relaxing against his ornate carriage, watching the grumbling matrons, he barely concealed his laughter. He had come looking for mischief, this one, and as Pandora stumbled into view, Andy feared he had found it.

"Go get your sister," she hissed. The twins would not waste themselves on the first pretty face to come their way; they had come for Fairbright. "I want you both with me. They might call our name at any moment."

Bess snorted. "We won't go anywhere for a good, long time."

"And why not? I see Miriam Dennison going in, and she arrived in the carriage before us."

Bess shook her head like a mother loathe to disappoint her child. "Because she's her ladyship's favorite, is why. Everyone else gets in by the size of their purse."

"They are taking bribes?"

"It is done all the time in town," M interjected anxiously. "The servants all expect them."

"A gratuity, perhaps, but not this. I can't believe Fairbright permits so tasteless a procedure. Where the de . . . is he?"

"No one seems to know. And Lady Sarah, Bess has heard, is absolutely livid about his absence."

Lady Sarah was not alone in this. Thinking of the darling dinner gowns, growing more and more crumpled, Andy in turn grew more and more miffed. First impressions meant all, she had drilled into the girls, but at this rate, the twins could as well bid their first impression, not to mention meal, farewell. All because, like her father, Fairbright was too self-centered to see to his obligations.

"Whoa, miss, where are you going?"

"To talk to someone," she said distractedly, trying to loosen Bess's grasp. "This confusion cannot continue."

"Andy, no," M protested gently. "We are guests here. You mustn't interfere."

"Go retrieve your sister." Efficient by need, Andy saw her intentions as altruistic, not meddlesome at all. If Fairbright's household was upside down, and she knew how to set it right again, logic decreed that she do so. "Bess, go with her and drag P back if you must. I want all three of you waiting beside this carriage when I return."

Shaking off the hand, and whatever doubts her sister had instilled, Andy marched to the steps. A lone servant in respendent black and silver livery stood there directing the others. She reasoned he must be in charge.

He was rapidly pocketing a wad of notes as he turned to her. His eager, unfolding fingers revealed a print-stained palm. It took but one look at her dreary gown for his hand to close up again like a clam.

"The entrance you seek is in the rear," he said with an oily smile, before turning to bow to his next customer.

Stunned, Andy could only stare at the woman now placing several crisp notes in his palm. It did not help that the newcomer was ravishing, sporting self-confidence with the same flair she wore her superbly cut clothes. Search though she might, Andy could find not a speck of dust on the impeccable black linen nor a single blond hair out of place. Still a paragon, she acceded grudgingly, for all that Elysse Farrington was well past the first bloom.

"Richard isn't expecting me," the woman drawled with a conspiratorial smile. "I thought I might surprise him."

"I daresay he shall be delighted, Lady Parsett. I will see you have the room of your choice." The man, with hand still extended, returned the smile.

"Dear Lot," Elysse sighed. Patting another crisp note into his palm, she sailed off into the house.

Andy didn't know which unsettled her more: Elysse's presence, or the way she'd said "Richard." *Her Richard?* In that case, he must be higher born than Andy had wanted to believe. Given his cultured speech and confident bearing, she granted he might be an impoverished cousin. As such, he'd be fair game for the greedy Lady Parsett. Cut from the same mold as Cousin Terese, Elysse liked to play. And Richard, quite clearly, had been marked as her new toy.

Someone should warn him, Andy thought. He must know that once Elysse had her fun, she would leave him. Just as she'd done with poor Geoff.

Shying away from the unpleasant memory, she decided someone as hardworking as Richard deserved better than the self-centered Elysse. He needed someone to mend his clothes and trim his dark brown hair to keep it from curling so audaciously, albeit adorably, at his collar. Someone able to tease out the occasional smile. Considering the one he'd given her, Andy felt he could indulge in more of them.

At her side, Lot clapped his hands, sending all remaining servants scurrying after Elysse. As none remained to deal with the other guests, among which her sisters numbered, Andy's waning temper snapped. "Of all the inconsiderate, ill-managed affairs . . ."

She could have been invisible. Lot certainly seemed to think so.

She raised her voice. "It might speed things if instead of sending all the servants off with each guest, leaving most with nothing more to do than fight over who shall open the door, you could send the idlers to those who need them."

She knew he had heard, but only by the tightening of his lips. They were not nice lips.

"Perhaps I should speak to his lordship? Tell me, does he know you've been fleecing his guests?"

Rapidly pocketing his ill-gotten gains, Lot schooled himself into the picture of outraged dignity. "How dare you imply such a thing!"

Noticing how many had gathered to listen, Andy

wondered the same. She glanced up to see a parted curtain in the window above. A blue-veined hand, undoubtedly belonging to Lady Sarah, held it open. Cringing, Andy imagined that lady's opinion of so rag-mannered a scene.

Yet though she should feel abashed, should apologize and even retreat, the thought of being watched and judged stiffened her spine. Hot, tired, and still smarting from the inevitable comparison to Elysse, Andy decided she was not about to knuckle under to anyone.

"I dare," she said, "because I happen to be one of those guests."

"You are not the temporary housekeeper?" Though taken aback, Lot recovered quickly. "A guest, madam? Then perhaps you will be kind enough to show me your name on this list?"

How dare he mistake her for a servant, she ranted inwardly, carefully avoiding the fact that her name was *not* upon his list. Stiffened with Gratham pride, refusing to admit she was merely a chaperon, she glared at his chest. "Either you move us all into the house at once, sir, or I shall go straight to his lordship."

She fully expected the lips to curl further, but to her surprise, they fell open in a startled O. Too late, she heard the hush around her. Even before she turned, she knew she would find Fairbright at the door. She did not, however, expect to find Just-call-me-Richard there.

"My lord," Lot wheezed. "I, uh . . . we, uh . . ."

"I heard." As the brown gaze flicked from the butler to her, Andy shut her jaw with a click. "I daresay half of England did. Shall we have mercy on the more sensitive ears, Mrs. Morton, and continue this discussion in the privacy of my study?"

"*Your* study?" She looked up from the gleaming buckles of his shoes, past the silk stockings, the buff-colored breeches and superfine jacket, to a face haughty with disdain. Her own anger, once so fortifying, vanished in a flash. "Oh, my. Then you are . . ."

He dipped into a mocking bow. "The Earl of Fairbright, at your command."

CHAPTER
4

Facing his lordship across a broad, intimidating desk, Andy knew she had never met anyone she was less likely to command. This haughty aristocrat before her, as implacable as he was impeccable, left her wondering if perhaps she had merely imagined the man upon the hill.

The once unruly hair sat in obedient elegance, as if aware of the folly in resisting his will. Crisp and white, his now flawless collar glistened against the sun-darkened skin. His even whiter cravat tumbled grace-fully down to a waistcoat of subtle blue brocade, which lay beneath a jacket of a darker hue. This last was cut to within a breath of him, as were his breeches, leaving little to imagine about the impressive form beneath.

The room, in contrast, was impossibly shabby. The man might be of the first stare, but the gleaming black of his shoes pointed out how the carpet had long since faded, and the starch in his linen merely accentuated the wear in the scarlet drapes. The rest of the furnishings were sparse, the lone ornaments being a desk lamp, a portrait over the mantel, and a chipped cage in the corner, from which could be heard the incessant chirping of a tiny bird. Given the opulent wealth displayed in the entrance foyer, Andy found the room as confusing as its owner.

How the devil could he be Fairbright? She could have sworn she heard those tattlemongers in Hookham's Library say the earl's name was Reginald.

"Please take a seat, Mrs. Morton. I will ring for refreshments."

"No, thank you." This lord-of-the-manor attitude must have been donned with the clothes, she scoffed. The more she thought of her careless speech on the hill, and the way he'd tricked her into feeling sorry for him, how he'd allowed—no, encouraged—her to continue, the more she bristled at his polished manners now.

"I shall sit," she said stiffly, "but do not take the staff from their work on my account. Half your guests will be sleeping in the drive as it is."

"Lot served my cousin for years. I daresay he knows what he's doing."

"Oh, yes, I'll grant you that. *I* would dare to say he could retire after this day's work."

"You are quite outrageous, you know." His voice was deceptively soft. "Hardly what one expects from a meek, penniless widow."

Andy plopped into the nearest chair. Its high back and deep sides all but engulfed her. As she defiantly dug her elbows into its arms, a wad of stuffing squirted free to land in her lap.

"Still, whatever Lot's faults," he continued in that same soft tone, "I fear he is right. Your name does not appear on the list."

Before Andy could protest, there was a banging on the floorboards behind her. "And what are you doing hiding in here?" demanded a querulous voice by the door.

Recognizing Lady Sarah's sharp tones, Andy felt like

a naughty child caught in a prank. She huddled deeper into the chair.

"Andrea Morton, may I present my aunt, the dowager Lady Sarah? But then, you two must already have met, no?"

Reluctantly, Andy rose to curtsey. "How nice to see you again, Lady Sarah."

The dowager gave a stiff nod, then promptly ignored her. "You should be out with your guests, Richard. They are making a great deal of noise."

"And who is to blame for that? Where are the servants you promised to provide?"

"Apparently delayed." The dowager edged forward, cane extended, and the earl sidestepped neatly as it came down onto the floor. "Do not assume it relieves you of your promise, boy. You gave your word to abide by our bargain."

"And so I will, madam. I could hope you would do the same." He nodded toward the painting over the fire-place.

At first glance, Andy thought it to be a portrait of a younger Richard, so devastating was that smile, but the powdered wig and long waistcoat belonged to a prior age.

"The portrait will be moved," Lady Sarah sniffed, "the moment a servant is available for the task. They are all currently occupied with your guests."

"As am I." Face stiffly set, the earl took his aunt by the elbow to steer her toward the door. "If you will excuse us, Mrs. Morton and I are in the midst of a discussion."

Andy, intimidated by the considering gaze now directed her way, sank down in the chair. This sent her ladyship's regard back to her nephew. He was not quick enough, this time, to avoid being skewered in the chest with her cane. "Miriam's been asking after you, boy."

"You, madam, are as transparent as the glass on this

door." With a weariness indicative of long practice, he eased the cane down and nudged his aunt into the hall.

"You know my wishes, Richard."

"And you know mine."

Watching their exchange, Andy tried to piece together the snips of gossip. Reginald must have been the cousin killed in the curricle race. Richard would thus be the one left at the altar. How Elysse must be kicking herself, now that he was the earl. Easy to guess why she was here then, but did those wishes of his coincide with hers?

Impossible to know. The man was a walking paradox. Though plainly upset with his aunt, his stroll remained maddeningly aloof as he went to his desk. "We appear to have a problem," he said as he snatched up a piece of paper. "As I was saying, your name is not upon this list."

Odious man. "Of course not. I am here as a chaperon. To my sisters. Check your list again and you will find the names of Amanda and Pandora Gratham."

"A chaperon, you say? You know, you could have spared us both a great deal by explaining this earlier."

"I might have, had you introduced yourself when we met. Instead of trying to trick me."

"Do you suggest I may have *cheated*, Mrs. Morton?" He eyed her over the paper. "My, my, there does seem to be a bit of that going around."

Abashed, Andy fell back into the seat. Another wad of stuffing tumbled to her lap.

"I was wrong to say that," she apologized, clutching the wad in her fists, "but please don't blame my sisters. They deserve to be judged on their own merits. I beg you, do not exclude them from your hunt."

"How prettily you plead for them." His gaze turned hard and assessing. Andy turned to the more important task of poking the wadding back into its hole. "Am I expected to believe you have no designs of your own?"

Dressed like this? she thought. "Rest easy, my lord. Your person is safe from me."

He did not seem easier. Indeed, his brows gathered in a sharp, dark V. "I can take care of my person; I am more concerned with my purse. You did declare yourself a pauper; I can only assume your sisters are likewise destitute?"

"Not precisely." She crossed her fingers in her lap. What was one more lie at this point? "They each have a small jointure. Besides, it is one's lineage that matters, is it not, rather than the size of one's fortune?"

"How naive of you." He set the paper down, knocking over a row of books. Muttering under his breath, the earl slammed each shut and righted them, before coming to stand before the desk. He leaned against it, inches from her, arms folded at his chest. "Do go on, though. You were describing your lineage?"

She sat as straight as the dilapidated chair would allow. "Before his untimely death, our father was the Earl of Huxworth."

"*Gambling Gerry?* Why, he—" He stopped abruptly, a futile attempt at tact. Gerry had certainly never exercised such discretion. "I never knew the man had daughters."

"He was neither pleased with nor proud of the fact." Andy snapped without thinking. Just thinking of her father was guaranteed to set her off. "Gerry wanted a son, you see. One could get along best with him by acting like one."

"Ah, I begin to see why four Seasons were necessary."

How dare he be amused. She stood, hands clasped at her sides, facing him squarely. "I know how to behave, sir. I can be quite ladylike when I must."

"A pity I was fighting on the Peninsula during your time in London. As diverting as Napoleon's antics were,

I imagine watching you 'behave' would be far more entertaining."

"You would not have had the opportunity, sir. We moved at the outermost fringe of society since my cousin Terese Dumont thought us too provincial to venture into the ton."

"Terese Dumont?" He smiled suddenly, and leaned closer. "I must say, I find myself curious. It does not seem like the Terese *I* knew to choose a pauper for you."

Too late, Andy realized that she had let her temper and pride get the best of her, that she had blurted out far more than she wished the man to know. "Mr. Morton was not a pauper," she tried to backtrack, sinking further into her chair. "Not then. He, er, was in trade, you see, and—"

"Trade!" One would think he'd been handed a bag of gold the way he beamed. "I see," he said, leaning closer still. "Then he left his business to someone else?"

"There, er, was nothing to leave." She was suddenly all too aware of how near he was, how his smile distorted her thinking. He seemed to be leading up to something, but her flustered brain could not see what it could be. And while part of her mind urged her to back away, to run away, another part goaded her closer to that wonderful smile. "He—he gambled," she said distractedly. "Heavily."

"Just like Gerry? When one considers your past, Mrs. Morton, it's a wonder you haven't sworn off men altogether."

Once again, the mere mention of her father stiffened her spine. "Oh, but I have," she snapped, eyes flashing as she edged backward. "I want nothing to do with the self-centered beasts."

Though the earl did not move any closer, his broadening grin made it seem as if he had. "Even if another were to offer, you would still refuse him?"

"I would."

"Even if he were an exceptional find? A—let us say—a catch?"

"Curiosity might compel me to ask why he should single me out when I have nothing to offer in return, but then I would refuse him." By this time, Andy had edged back so far, she was up against the seat of the chair. She sat, arms folded defiantly—or perhaps protectively—in front of her.

He shook his head. "The more I think on this, the more I wonder how I can sit back and let you play the stuffy chaperon." He leaned back to retrieve a sheet of paper from his desk. "Indeed, if my conscience is to allow me a wink of sleep tonight, your name simply must be on this list."

"You can't be serious!"

"Never more so. Is that Andrea with one *n*, or two?"

"No, wait." The prospect of going about with all those exquisitely dressed girls, especially Elysse Farrington, filled Andy with alarm. Yet how could she admit such vanity to this man? "Do think," she tried instead. "It would hardly be proper. I'm in mourning."

"Propriety would hardly frown upon joining in a small country to-do."

"But please, I am nothing like your other guests. I haven't their manners, or—or polish. They will be outraged. Only think of your aunt's reaction."

"Yes." He could have swallowed the canary, chirping so obliviously in the corner. "Pity, but it cannot be helped."

"You don't understand. My sisters—they must have a chaperon."

"I will speak to Agatha Dennison. I daresay she can look after you all."

As if she were drowning, Andy grasped at her last straw. "There is a chance I might win. What then?"

To her amazement, and further chagrin, he merely grinned. "The rules might compel me to offer, but as you will find when you read them, you are under no obligation to accept. Relax, Mrs. Morton. You might even have fun."

"Fun? My, but you *are* arrogant."

The grin vanished. "Must I point out that you are a guest in my home?"

"As effectively as you might play lord of the manor, sir, let me point out that England is a free country. You cannot force me to comply."

"Too true. But I can ask you to leave and if your sisters are worth a twig, I'm certain they'd wish to go with you. Which is a pity, for I was quite looking forward to meeting them."

"Why, you scoundrel. This is blackmail!"

"As long as we understand each other." Setting the list on the desk with a cool deliberation, he rose to his feet and crossed to the bell rope. With a quick yank, he turned to face her with his most disdainful air. "We are to assemble in the drawing room after dinner, at which time I assume Lady Sarah wishes to explain the rules of the hunt. I shall look forward to seeing you there."

He crossed the room to bow before the door. Speechless, Andy whirled in the chair. Miserable, underhanded wretch. Having manipulated her into this awkward situation, he now thought he could so rudely dismiss her? Irked beyond measure, she jumped to her feet, more of the chair's insides falling unheeded to the rug.

"Mary will show you to your rooms," he continued from the doorway. "When one considers the rest of my cousin's staff, she's the closest to efficiency I can offer."

"You will persist in this despite my protests?" Andy could scarcely contain her anger as she joined him. "Have you no heart?"

"Ask any of those gabblemongers you listen to in London. I daresay they will swear I never had one."

"Before I am done," she told him through her teeth, "you will rue the day you included me."

"Yes. I daresay I shall."

Something in his tone made her pause. Gazing up, Andy saw a softening in his eyes, a hint of doubt and perhaps self-derision, but then the maid appeared and the earl turned as stone-faced as ever. "Mary, please show Mrs. Morton to her room."

"That is kind of you, my lord," she said, determined to be just as falsely civil, "but my sisters must be settled first. They'll need to share a room."

"The Spanish have a saying, Mrs. Morton: 'My house is your house.' Please, feel free to settle wherever you must."

He gave one last insincere smile, and while he did not actually slam the door in her face, Andy was left with the distinct impression he had.

Strangely, she felt a vague sense of loss. No, she told herself sternly. The man on the hill existed only in her imagination. Just-call-me-Richard was in truth the earl, and every bit as impossible as she'd portrayed.

Squaring her shoulders, she led the maid to the twins, grumbling about strutting males and their overbearing arrogance. So he meant to use her, did he? It took little genius to guess his intent. She'd seen the exchange with his aunt, his subsequent need to thwart her. Andy, with her colorful antecedents and expressed distaste for marriage, must have seemed like the reddest of herrings he'd ever dangled on a hook.

Well, he would soon learn Andrea Gratham didn't dangle for anyone!

On the other side of the door, Richard eyed the tufts scattered across his carpet. Annoyed, he leaned down to retrieve them. At this rate, his favorite chair would soon be reduced to its frame.

And while he could not in all justice blame the young widow for its decomposition, his frustration must be focused somewhere. After all, the woman made herself a most convenient target. And an even better pawn for his plans.

Going to the desk, he grabbed the invitation list. He'd best scribble in her name now, so his aunt would be certain to see it. Too bad he couldn't pen in the chit's attributes, for he couldn't have done better had he improvised them himself: Gambling Gerry's daughter, Terese Dumont's protégée, and, best yet, a husband in trade.

And since Lady Sarah had invited her, she had only herself to blame if he showed a direct preference for the young widow's company. Add that to the outrageous background and deplorable manners, and his aunt would be reduced to outright apoplexy when the woman won the hunt.

Andrea Morton must win, he swore, by fair means or foul. Not only was she the sole entrant guaranteed to reject him, but his aunt's relief would then be so great, it would put a stop to any further talk of marriage.

As if he'd already been handed the reprieve, he went gleefully to greet his guests.

He'd taken but two steps into the hallway when his canary erupted into warbled hysteria. He turned back, unable to remember the last time he'd fed it. Guilt prompted this action, but so did a spurt of empathy. He knew just how it felt to be caged in, able only to squawk in protest.

Opening the cage, he paused for an uncomfortable moment, remembering the look in Mrs. Morton's eyes. She had seemed as frightened and as helpless as this bird, the day he'd found it abandoned by Elysse in his rooms.

But Andrea Morton was not a bird, he forced himself to recall. Like Elysse, she was a woman. And as such, not to be pitied, or even trusted, for a moment.

Odd, though, how she'd sought nothing for herself. All her energy had been focused on the twins. Indeed, she'd been more concerned over her precious sisters than in ever becoming his wife. Deuced insulting, when one thought of it, needing to force the chit to participate. The more Richard dwelled upon this, the more irritated he became, and the more justified he felt in using her to thwart his aunt.

As he slammed the cage door shut, the canary screeched all the louder, though this time not out of hunger. From the day he'd given it to her, the bird shrieked whenever Elysse entered the room.

"Richard, darling," she gushed in her soft, sensual drawl. "It's been so long."

Not long enough, he thought. There were many residual feelings the years had yet to erase, and the sight of her evoked every one. She still looked lovely, confound her, and seemed twice as aware of it.

She swept into the room, filling it with her expensive scent. "I couldn't believe the talk when they said you'd buried yourself here. I wonder what can be the attraction."

"I am the earl now. I have responsibilities."

"My, but you sound the absolute bore. I'd hoped we could have fun together, like old times. Or have you forgotten?"

"The last time we spoke, I believe, 'forgetting' was your idea. Can I be blamed if I took your words to heart?"

A tiny smile played at those full red lips. "You also took my bird, I see. You can't have forgotten it all." She glided forward, her face a seduction in itself.

"I could hardly leave it to starve." Annoyed at the admission, Richard went behind his desk, using its huge expanse as a shield.

"You're angry," she pouted. "It was ghastly of me to come without an invitation, I know, but surely you never meant to exclude me from your hunt?"

"The hunt was my aunt's idea. Plead with her."

If she noticed his curtness, she chose to ignore it. "Considering my recent bereavement, I suppose I should have stayed at home. But it sounds such a lark, Richard. Just like before." She fluttered those long silky lashes meaningfully. "Let the old crones twitter, I say. As long as a good friend needs me, my participation is proper enough. After all, this is but a small, country affair."

A pretty speech, and one he could hardly refute. Hadn't he spouted the same to Mrs. Morton? "Propriety?" he snapped instead. "Since when do you concern yourself with such a thing?"

She smiled up at him, far from proper now. The expression was familiar, and each memory it invoked was a vivid one. A good portion of his wildness, if the truth were known, had come at her instigation.

"Do not devastate me, darling. Do say I might join in. Oh, is this the list? I shall just jot down my name."

She peeled off her gloves, the action slow and sensual. Another rush of memories swept over him. A sense of fatalism replaced his first impulse of snatching both pen and list from her well-formed hands. Once Elysse got a bee in her bonnet, he well knew, it was the very devil to dislodge it.

Let her join in, he decided. Next to Mrs. Morton, Elysse had to be the second best guarantee to appalling his aunt. Besides, whatever her faults, Lady Parsett's shapely form was an infinitely preferable view to the uninspired dowd that was Miriam Dennison.

Deliberately displaying a great deal of that form as she bent over the desk, Elysse worked her old magic. Grinning, Richard decided that the next two weeks might prove diverting yet. Made quite a contrast, Elysse and Mrs. Morton did, one that might yet work in his favor.

For the first time since his aunt presented the idea, he began to think this hunt might be fun at that.

CHAPTER
5

"But I think Lord Foxley would be perfect."

"Hush, do you wish Bess to know of our plans?" P glanced over her shoulder at their housekeeper-turned-abigail. P could not help it, could she, if her gaze slid past to the young gentleman grinning behind her? "Forget Foxley. I've found someone else. Lord Bellington."

M shook her blond curls, careful to keep her voice low as she eyed Bellington. "But P, we know nothing about him. All the gossip I've heard says he's a determined rake. Is that what we want for our dear Andy?"

"I know he can be splendid fun," P countered irritably. "Isn't that the sole reason we agreed to this silly hunt? So Andy might enjoy herself for a change?"

For all her gentle mannerisms, M had a stubborn streak of her own. "*And* so we might find her a husband. A strong, capable, sensible man to take care of her, the way she has always cared for us."

"Pooh, M. Your Foxley is far too young."

"No more so than your Bellington." At her sister's

upraised brow, she colored slightly. "He told me they were school chums. When he retrieved my bonnet. It blew off, and, well, oh, do stop staring at me so."

"Amanda Gratham, were you playing the flirt?"

"I was not! And I will not suffer your teasing, P. Not when there is Andy's future to discuss. I will have you know she scowled, the moment she saw your Lord Bellington."

"Never say." There was a slight upward curving of Pandora's lips before she schooled them into a scowl of her own. "It matters little. You know Andy compares every man to Geoff. For her own good, we simply must find her a husband. And I think Lord Bellington is the logical choice."

"Lord Foxley," insisted M, also frowning. She cast a glance to where said gentleman chatted with dreadful Elysse Farrington. She suffered a pang. Though not for herself, of course. She'd earmarked Foxley for Andy; she was not about to let that harridan snatch another man away from her.

Pursing her lips, she looked P in the eye. "I say we push both gentlemen her way and let Andy decide for herself."

"Why, M, what a splendid idea. And I say there is no time like the present to start. I think I shall go speak with Lord Bellington now."

"Oh, but P, here comes Andy. And she does not look one whit happy."

M, as anyone in the family would explain, had a knack for understatement. Looking at her older sister's face, P was glad she'd had no time to act on her impulse.

Aside from a curt "Come with me," Andy said nothing. Eyeing each other in bewilderment, the twins kept silent as they fell in step behind a pretty little maid named Mary.

Chatting airily, Mary described the rest of the staff as they climbed the stairs. Bess, uncommonly quiet herself, stopped her in mid-sentence. *Martha* Bumfrey was the ailing housekeeper? she demanded of the girl. Learning that it was indeed the same Martha she'd served with so many years ago, their makeshift abigail decamped, hurrying belowstairs with Mary to see what she could do for poor Martha's back.

P could not stifle a smile. It would be far easier to execute their plan for Andy without Bess and her overbearing common sense. She could not wait to have M alone, so they could begin plotting what to do at dinner tonight.

"Dratted man," Andy muttered as she ushered them into a huge, well-appointed bedroom of coral and white.

"Who?" P asked softly, crossing her fingers behind her back. How discouraging, if Lord Bellington had again set such a scowl on her face. "Who is a dratted man?"

Andy whirled to face her. "That blasted Fairbright; do you know what he's done?"

Both girls shook their heads, each fearing the worst.

"He's forced me to join his absurd hunt, that's what." With another huff, Andy stomped past them into the room.

Sparing her sister a hopeful glance, M hurried behind her. "But this is wonderful news," she gushed. "It means you shall be able to meet . . . I mean, well, you'll always be near to help us."

"Yes, you are ever so more clever," P piped in. "And we know how you do so love a puzzle. With your help, we cannot possibly lose."

Smiling, Andy turned to tenderly brush the hair from P's face. "As if you needed my help to win. A man need but gaze into your faces for you both to be wed within the year."

As much as P thrived upon hearing such praise, she could not forget their primary goal. "But what of you, Andy? Isn't it time you sought a husband for yourself?"

It was as if a great, wide wall fell down between them. Tight-lipped, Andy went to the door. "Bess will see to your baths as soon as she's seen to Mrs. Bumfrey. Your luggage should be along shortly. Remember, we agreed on the silk gowns for tonight. M in green; P in yellow. If you need me, I shall be upstairs."

"Upstairs?" the twins groaned in unison. "So far away?"

"It is where I belong. With the *other* chaperons."

P could not hide her dismay. "Oh, but Andy, we want you here. With . . . with us."

She softened for a moment, her face revealing just how lovely she could be in the right clothes. "Don't be silly. I shall be near whenever you need me."

"You'll be going to dinner with us, then?" M pressed.

"You can't expect us to manage alone," P added.

"Girls, think. I haven't a thing to wear to a formal dinner."

Again the twins exchanged glances. They were prepared for this. Hadn't they delayed their fittings for this very purpose? By mutual—albeit silent—consent, P spoke. "There are a few gowns not yet altered. You and Cousin Terese are of a size; why not wear one of hers?"

"I . . . I . . ."

"Oh, please. We'll be ever so frightened without you."

"Please, Andy. We need you."

Magic words, guaranteed to succeed. Andy might continue to protest, but each offering grew more feeble until they were hurrying her off with her solemn promise to meet them again at dinner.

Alone, the twins turned to each other with mischievous grins. "Next, we must get her into new chambers," P said with a giggle. "It will be far simpler to set the gentlemen in her way if they needn't climb all those stairs."

"I can't wait for her to meet him," M sighed.

P flopped down on the four-poster bed and stared dreamily at the ceiling. "Isn't it wonderful? By this time next year, we shall be calling her Lady Bellington."

"Foxley," her sister muttered under her breath.

Unaware of their plans, an impatient Andy waited in the kitchen for Bess to return. She had come down quite some time ago, hoping Bess would know the where-abouts of the sash and gloves to match the gown she must wear, only to learn the woman had agreed to serve as housekeeper in her good friend Martha's stead. As it was dinnertime, one kitchen crisis after another had led to a considerable delay.

Helping where she could, as it was not in her nature to stand idle, Andy had no time to remember her promise to the twins until now, in the relative peace and quiet of the after-dinner lull. Not that she doubted their success, but she did so hate to disappoint them. Her promise to meet them was, she admitted ruefully, the sole reason she continued to wait for that sash and gloves.

Behind her, the clock struck the hour. The pie should be done, she thought, her innate efficiency assuming control. Reaching for oven mitts, she removed the pie, lifting the covered dish holding the earl's dinner into the cavernous oven to warm.

She hoped Mrs. Bumfrey was right and this food pacified him. Though she might remain opposed to the man's tactics, and vehemently determined to avoid his hunt, she had no wish to disrupt his life. Fighting for one's goals was one thing; depriving a man of his dinner was quite another.

Not that he would ever learn she'd prepared it. The moment Bess returned with the sash, she planned to slip into the dress, dash down to the parlor for the evening's events, and act as if she'd been part of his dratted hunt all along.

There's Bess now, she thought, hearing footsteps.

Setting the pie on the table before her, she looked up as the door burst open.

Leaving his male guests to their port, Richard followed their female counterparts from the dining hall. His intent was not to join the ladies, however, but to put a halt to whatever that blasted Morton woman thought she was up to now.

Dinner had been an orchestrated effort to punish him, he decided as he marched to the kitchen. However skillfully prepared and incessantly praised, the roast pheasant had been accompanied by every other dish he was known to despise. And it was no small coincidence, in his opinion, that Andrea Morton had set up camp in his kitchen.

Cheeky woman. Strolling into his house, taking control of it, deliberately doing her utmost to irk him. If she weren't precisely what he needed to defy his aunt, he'd have both her and her precious sisters tossed out on their pretty little ears at once.

Shoving through the kitchen doors, he was forestalled by the temptation of a large, steaming pie. As he inhaled the heady aroma of baked apple with cinnamon to spare, he forgot his mission. He weighed his chances of escaping, unseen, with the whole of it in his hands.

Until he noticed the figure behind it. He felt like a child again, caught in the act. Kindly Mrs. Bumfrey would have offered a taste of whatever he tried to pilfer, but there would be no such generosity today. One glance at that unsmiling face reminded him that Martha Bumfrey was no longer ruling the kitchen. Somehow, Mrs. Morton was.

"I must say," he said dryly. "In telling you my house was yours, I did not expect you to take me so literally."

"But I—"

"Your culinary skills are matchless," he continued. "Or so I am told. Pity I can't judge for myself, as I have this adverse reaction to pheasant. Not that you could know that though, could you?"

"You're hungry," she stated, making it sound like a philosophical observation or the diagnosis a physician might render. "It's as well Mrs. Bumfrey warned us."

She turned to the stove, leaving Richard in a state of such bewilderment, he quite forgot any reproach he meant to make.

"Here," she said softly as she returned to set a plate before him. "Perhaps this will have you feeling more the thing."

Richard eyed the food with suspicion. Next to a slab of rich, red beef sat a pile of steaming potatoes, a row of glazed carrots, and stem after stem of generously buttered asparagus. They were all his favorites, as any servant in the house could have told her.

"Go on; it won't bite," she teased. "You must be famished."

To Richard's shame, his belly grumbled. "You must think me monumentally gap-skulled, madam. This was the original menu, was it not? I can guess why you changed it."

"Oh, no! I didn't . . . that is . . . oh, please, sit and eat while I explain."

Though he was well aware of the adage about a woman's power over a man's stomach, the scents drifting up from the plate overcame his better judgment. Sitting slowly, his wary eyes never leaving her face, he watched for any signs of triumph. He would not put it past the woman to poison him.

But as one bite led to another, he no longer cared. For all her kindliness, Mrs. Bumfrey had at best been a competent cook. This female so eagerly watching his every bite could rival the most expensive chef in London.

Drawing in a breath, she sat beside him. "We did not,

as you seem to believe, deliberately set out to starve you."

Busy with his meal, Richard could only raise a brow. She blushed, then flashed an impish grin.

"I will not say I wouldn't have, had I the time to think of it, but necessity, and not I, forced the change in menu. There was an appalling lack of beef, you see, while thanks to Fr . . . er, someone's poaching, there was pheasant to spare."

Richard nearly choked. "Poaching? God spare me, where?"

"I assure you, the birds came from your own lands. Though I did need to promise the boy immunity. Under the solemn oath he would never poach from you again."

A futile promise, Richard thought. Reggie had never been able to stop the wily Freddie Perkins, not even with all the Fairbright wealth behind him. But then, his cousin had never wrestled the ill-gotten gains from the boy, either.

As if seeing his doubts, and hoping to exploit them, she smiled. "I must also warn, you owe quite a sum for the rest of the meal. For a man expecting so many guests, my lord, you were woefully unprepared."

"Ah, but I wasn't," he said between bites. "Unprepared, perhaps, but I was not expecting guests. They were my aunt's idea."

"I see," said Mrs. Morton, absentmindedly slicing and then sliding over a piece of aromatic pie. "Then the staff was right about that."

It was unnerving, how servants learned each tiny detail, but it was positively terrifying to consider such knowledge in this woman's hands. How much had she gleaned in her short stint in his kitchens? Whatever it took, Richard decided, she must be removed from here at once.

He stood, sparing a last, regretful glance at the pie.

"The meal was superb, but I am neglecting my guests. Of which, I feel compelled to remind, you number."

"I need no reminders."

Richard bristled. Most women would sell their souls to be included. She needn't make it sound like a penance. "On the contrary, I believe you do. Or do you plan to play my housekeeper for the remainder of your visit?"

"Your . . . ?" She clamped her lips shut. Her eyes began to gleam. "Actually, though, becoming your housekeeper is not all that bad an idea."

It was the last straw. "Good Lord, woman, isn't that flying a bit too stiffly into the face of convention?" He thought, but did not say, "Even for you?"

She nonetheless answered him. "There is nothing the least conventional about me. Not my behavior, my upbringing, nor even my expectations. Can't you see? I'd be far happier here than prancing about with all those giggling girls."

"No one said you must prance, Mrs. Morton."

She inhaled deeply. "Listen to me. It could serve us both to advantage. Wouldn't it be ever more pleasant working with and not against each other?"

As she leaned closer, he caught the scent of apples. It struck him how well it suited her, this domesticity. She was quite pleasant, almost comfortable, here in his favorite room of the house. It might be kinder to her, not to mention his own creature comforts, to let her remain. Especially if her skills ran to cherry pie, as well.

But then Richard thought of those giggling, prancing girls, one of which would then maintain permanent residence in his life. "Too late," he said brusquely. "My aunt knows you're included. What do you think she'd say to finding you here? It's not quite the thing, you must know, taking charge of your host's kitchen. However much you wish to irk him."

"You can't think I—"

"I will overlook such unseemly behavior, Mrs. Morton, provided you now hurry to the gold drawing room, where my aunt waits to read the rules of the hunt. As I remember, you did assure me you knew how to act like a lady when you must?"

"I . . . I . . . ."

"As Lady Sarah won't begin until everyone is present, and since she is not known for her patience, I suggest you hurry. Else she'll set the footmen to scouring the halls for you."

She opened her mouth to protest, but clearly thought better of it. Spinning on a heel, she pushed through the door in a huff.

Watching her, slowly realizing how harsh he'd been, Richard pushed a hand through his hair. She'd done it again, he thought irritably. That harum-scarum female had goaded him into losing his temper.

He was about to go after her when a large, red-faced woman bustled into the room. "Where's An . . . er, Mrs. Morton?" she asked gruffly, before dropping into a belated curtsey and adding, "My lord."

"Mrs. Morton has gone to the gold drawing room," he snapped, hurrying past. "Where she belongs."

The woman glanced at the blue sash in her hands and sighed. "Too late, I am. And after I kept her waiting all this time. Never did have her dinner, poor dear, what with me busy so frantic to get the meal on the table."

"*You* cooked the meal?" Unsettled, Richard paused at the door. "Forgive me, but I don't believe I know who you are."

"Bess Jenkins, my lord. Standing in as housekeeper, I am, what with Martha being abed, and your kitchens being all in sixes and sevens."

"You? I was under the impression Mrs. Morton was acting in that capacity?"

"I should say not! A lady, that's what my girl is, as

fine as any you'll find. Not that she ain't fit to carry on the job, of course. Ran her father's house for years."

"But my dinner . . . the pie . . ."

"Heart of gold, that girl has. Wouldn't let anyone go a-starving. No matter if they deserve it or no."

Ignoring the pointed gaze, Richard left. Said dinner and pie were now creating a decided lump in his gut. It appeared he'd been somewhat hasty and perhaps unfair in his judgment. That had not been defiance he'd seen in her eyes as he chastised her, but affront. And perhaps hurt.

But drat the woman, why hadn't she spoken up? She'd stood there while he heaped on the abuse, letting him make a fool of himself. All to make him look bad, he didn't doubt. A carefully calculated scheme to force him to feel so much guilt, he'd relent and let her go her own way.

Manipulating him; just like his aunt.

Muttering under his breath, he stormed out of the kitchen. No female would get the best of him, he swore. He was master of this house.

And whatever it took, he'd remain master of this confounded hunt.

CHAPTER
6

Lady Sarah sat on the makeshift dais, surveying her guests, feeling altogether pleased with herself. There was nothing she enjoyed more than her own deviousness.

Her nephew, however, did not seem to be enjoying himself at all. Good, she chuckled. It was well past time Richard's routine was upset. He truly was getting to be a stick.

"And just what is so amusing?"

Such peevishness did not become Amelia. She should know Sarah would not reveal the name on her wager until the end of the hunt. These snits of hers would get her nowhere.

"Do look at Richard." The dowager nodded toward her nephew. "He doesn't look happy, does he?"

Moments earlier, Lady Parsett had sidled up to snatch his right arm. Urged on by her mother, Miriam Dennison now stomped up to secure a similar hold on his left.

"Poor dear. They will devour him. Oh, Sarah, how ever could you invite that awful Parsett woman?"

"Didn't. And Richard's included one more female, you know. Another widow. Oh, but then you've seen Mrs. Morton; she was shouting at Lot in the drive."

Amelia shuddered. "Dreadful scene. You should have sent her packing. She can't be quality."

"On the contrary. She's a Gratham. One of Gerry's brood."

"Gerry Gratham? Oh, Sarah, not *your* Gerry?"

"Of course not; it was the father I knew." Absurd, after all these years to feel that familiar pang. Sarah had made her choice and she had learned to be happy with it. "And he was hardly *my* Gerry," she snapped at Amelia. "Forget your silly romantic notions, and be advised: Richard insisted the chit be included."

"But why? She's not at all his sort."

Though she was not about to confide in Amelia, Sarah was likewise intrigued by her nephew's motives. And doubly determined to learn what they were.

The boy would bear watching.

Indeed unhappy, "the boy" was again feeling like a fish fighting the pull of the line. Being tugged about by these females had him wishing he'd stayed in the kitchen.

"Richard, darling," Elysse purred at his right. "We have been searching this age and more for you."

"Come, Dickon," Miriam insisted, proving she was not part of Elysse's *we* by towing him the opposite way. "We should take our place with your aunt."

"But of course we should. But first, Richard must see who I've found. Darling, doesn't Geoffrey look splendid?"

Risking his sleeves, Richard yanked free of both females to grasp his friend's hand. "Geoff, how good to see you," he said, meaning every word. Richard owed this man a debt of gratitude, for it had been upon Geoff's advice that he joined with Wellington after Elysse's jilting, an occupation more sensible than remaining to become the brunt of every *on-dit*.

"Richard, you old reprobate." Geoff pumped his hand, his slate-gray eyes twinkling with a familiar air of mischief. Always good for a laugh as Lord Lennox. "Sorry to hear about Reggie and all that, but I've always said you'd make a better earl. By the look of things, can't see a female here who won't have you now."

The gray eyes slid to Elysse, the taunt deliberate. The sorriest act in his life, Geoff had confessed long ago, was bringing Miss Farrington to Fairbright Manor. For from the start, Elysse had stalked a title. Hearts were mere stepping stones on her quest, Geoff claimed, his being her bottommost rung. Richard's came next, as the means to her true prize, his cousin, the earl. And when Reggie proved stubbornly immune to marriage, Parsett became her only logical move.

All true, Richard supposed, but he had no wish to discuss it now in front of his guests. Excusing themselves from the ladies, no easy task in itself, he led Geoff to a less audible portion of the room.

"Sorry about that, old chap." Geoff beamed, giving lie to the words. "But she does mean to have you, you know."

There was something so damned likeable about the man, Richard could never stay irked for long. "Then she has competition," he said with a reluctant grin. "My aunt seems set on Miriam. I daresay she concocted this absurd hunt just to steer the blasted female my way."

"Cry off, then, for heaven's sake."

"Can't. I gave my word."

"Not the word of a Fairbright? Lud, Richard, then you are doomed. Is there anything I can do?"

"I am inclined to doubt so; I've been condemned by a jury of female peers. The Tribunal—" he paused to gesture at his aunt and her two elderly friends—"is determined to see me wed."

Geoff gave a mock shudder. "Then you are good and truly doomed. What can I offer but my condolences?"

"I'm glad you asked. Actually, I need information."

Widening his eyes in expectancy, Geoff reached into a pocket for a gaudy silver snuffbox. Neither of them used the stuff, but it was so like Geoff to carry on the pretense.

"As I recall," Richard continued, stifling a smile, "your uncle's estate sat in the vicinity of Gambling Gerry's place. Perchance, have you ever met his daughters?"

"Bounced about with the chits in my youth, actually. Had an incurably adorable mother; thought it quaint to rhyme their names. Made for quite a mouthful. Interested in one, sly devil? Must be Candy. Or Randy." His grin dissolved, the gray eyes narrowed. "Never say it's Andy?"

Confused by the litany, for the names meant nothing to him, Richard shook his head. "The twins, actually. They're on the guest list, but I've yet to make their acquaintance. I'd hoped you might point them out."

"The twins? Lud, Richard, you've sunk to robbing the cradle. Damned if I don't feel compelled to go to your aunt. Though it's all her fault, I daresay."

"I don't mean to offer for them, dolt. It's mere curiosity. I've been told they are quite lovely."

"True. Given your penchant for intellect, though, I must express my doubt that they've a brain to share between them. More Jamie's and Adam's sort, I would think."

He gestured to Foxley and Bellington, both exerting their charm on a pair of matched beauties. One glance, and Richard understood the woman's pride in her sisters. And her need to keep watch over them.

As if planned, Mrs. Morton chose that moment to appear in the doorway. Bad enough his gaze should drift there at that precise moment, but it seemed determined to remain. He watched her wince as she noticed his aunt, narrow her eyes as they found Elysse, and lift her chin as she spied the twins. But the most revealing gaze of all came when her eyes met his. There was no mistaking the hostility glittering there.

Pointedly looking past him, she transformed before his eyes. Whatever starch animosity had loaned now drained off with astonishing speed. Face white, she hurried off to a darkened corner of the room.

No longer able to see her through the rows of seated guests, Richard cursed softly. Now what had he done to cause her distress? Had she guessed he'd meant to go to her? But how, when he had not realized it himself?

"Begging your pardon, my lord," Lot said at his elbow. "The Lady Sarah wishes you to join her."

He could hear Geoff's muttered "Doomed" behind him, a sentiment he shared as both Miriam and Elysse regained their holds on his sleeves.

Andy sat with a thud. In all her worst imaginings, she'd never anticipated meeting Geoffrey Stone, now Lord Lennox, here at the Fairbright hunt. Providence, if indeed it was divine, must be punishing her for pinching her cousin's clothes.

She had marched into the drawing room armed with resolve, for no man, be he earl or no, was about to tell Gerry Gratham's firstborn what she must do. If Fairbright insisted upon including her in this hunt, she'd vowed, she would become the most effusively giggling and prancing debutante it was ever his ill judgment to invite.

Such resolve was all well and good, but Geoff was here, and that changed everything.

Must he look so wonderful? she protested as her gaze wandered back to him. The auburn hair, which at nineteen had a tendency to poke up at odd angles, now sat with polished elegance upon his handsome head. There was something equally nice in the set of those shoulders, so neatly encased in his refined evening dress. He'd become quite the gentleman, she realized with a pang. Did he still play with that silly snuffbox she had given him one Christmas as a joke? Oh, the laughs they'd shared. The adventures. Until Elysse.

It was embarrassing, even now, to remember. How could she have hoped anyone as dashing as Geoff would choose her when the lovely Miss Farrington had flung her cap in his face? And when one had a father like Gambling Gerry Gratham.

Wincing, she recalled the last time she'd seen Geoff. Such hopes she'd had for that assembly, for all that it was a local affair and her dress was older than her own sixteen years. With a mother too busy to advise her and only the housemaids for example, she had not seen where her plan could go awry. She and Geoff had been childhood companions, nearly sweethearts; surely one simple kiss would fix his attentions back where they belonged?

She should have known his reaction by his reluctance to go outdoors with her, but she'd truly expected a declaration of love, if not marriage. As such, she'd been completely unprepared for the startled laughter in his eyes.

And if the private mortification were not enough, her father, dragging his intoxicated cronies outdoors to rehash the Battle of Culloden, chose that precise moment to stumble over them.

"Whad's this," Gerry had shouted. For all that his speech lacked clarity, it did not want for volume, drawing whoever might not have already gathered around them. "Unhand m'daughter, pup. Ye'll name the weddin day or ye'll name yer seconds."

"She grabbed me," Geoff blurted out, stepping away as if Andy had burned him.

"Corporal?"

Gerry, using the name he'd always called her, commanded no less than the truth. Mortified to the tips of her borrowed dancing slippers, Andy could only nod. A full round of chuckles erupted around her.

"Is Andy pestering poor Geoff again?" Her entrance perfectly timed, Elysse swept up to commandeer his sleeve. "Pathetic child, can't you ever leave him alone?"

This fueled a more boisterous round of mirth. Wanting to die, Andy turned to Geoff, only to watch him walk away with Elysse on his arm.

Gerry wandered off for a bottle, leaving her to face the snickers alone, an occupation that remained her lot for years to come. In London, the incident might have been quickly forgotten in lieu of another, but as so little ever happened in their quiet village, her fate was sealed. Andy became the village joke, and as such a matrimonial risk, for what man wished to ally himself with a perennial chuckle?

Which was as well, she'd oft repeated to herself, for her mother sickened soon after, and the care and welfare of her sisters must by need be her sole concern.

Something, she reminded herself sternly, she must not lose sight of now.

She scanned the room for her sisters. Finding them beside the two young gentlemen M had pointed out in the drive, she frowned. They should be with Fairbright.

She popped up to set things right, only to notice the hush. Apparently Lady Sarah had no need to speak; her very presence was enough to silence the room. Since everyone else seemed to have already done so, Andy sat back down.

A queen rising from her throne, the dowager used her cane like a scepter. "Welcome to Fairbright Manor," she pronounced after a lengthy pause, her gaze no less regal than her pose. "As I hope you are all well aware, you have been summoned for one purpose and one purpose alone. Fairbright must have an heir."

Andy was not the only one startled by such bluntness.

There was more than one indrawn breath, a titter or two, and a definite tightening of the earl's handsome face.

"At my age," the dowager went on, "I have neither time nor patience for roundaboutation. My only desire, my sole duty, is to see the line continue. A single-mindedness, I must warn, I expect in my nephew's bride. It is not enough to merely covet the title, you see; you must earn it!"

Throughout this speech, Andy studied the earl. Had he been aware of her scrutiny, he might have taken greater care to mask his emotions, for they were all there for the eye to see. His resentment, his frustration, and, yes, his embarrassment too. He must truly feel as if he were being auctioned off to the highest bidder. Relax, Andy could have told him; Elysse would top any bid.

"Hence the hunt," Lady Sarah continued, waving a rolled parchment. "To help you learn what being a Fairbright means, you will answer a series of questions about our family history. The rules are written down on this parchment, which I suggest you peruse at your leisure. I want no one coming to me later with complaints. Ignorance will not save you from being disqualified."

Her gaze swept the room, daring anyone to challenge her. "To be brief, then, each night as you sleep, a question concerning Fairbright history will be placed beneath your door. You will have until midnight of the same day to divine the correct answer and place it in the enameled box at the second story main landing. Those failing to submit correctly will be summarily excluded from the hunt."

She paused to smile, as if the prospect gave the utmost satisfaction. "There will be no exceptions, so do not bother to come sniveling to me about it. There can be only one winner, after all."

The room began to buzz. The dowager held up a hand for silence and was granted it at once. "It sounds too simple, you no doubt think. What is to prevent you all from winning? To insure against such an outcome, therefore, we've added a twist. What is the hunt, after all, without a quarry?"

Again she paused, this time for dramatic effect, and there wasn't a head in the room that didn't lean forward. In his lordship's case, however, there was a definite note of uneasiness in the pose.

"Your quarry, in this instance, shall be the Fairbright betrothal ring. It's an emerald, the gaudiest thing imaginable. As you answer each question, you will build your store of knowledge leading to its whereabouts. Be the first to find the emerald, and you shall win the right to wear it."

Again, Andy watched the earl. To say he was displeased would be an understatement. By the time his aunt finished with her "Happy hunting, ladies," he seemed ready to explode.

As much as Andy might have enjoyed witnessing their inevitable confrontation, two things prevented this. One was his lordship firmly removing his aunt from the room, and the other was the highly perceptible giggles from the twins.

"Doubloons?" she could hear P chirp. "Legendary treasure? Why, we'd rather hunt for that, wouldn't we, M?"

M, Andy saw, showed a gratifying reluctance. At least she glanced nervously about the room before nodding.

Andy started forward, knowing that as their older sister and erstwhile chaperon, it was her duty to take them to task at once. Unfortunately, two steps later, she noticed Geoff was dauntingly close. Not that she was frightened to face him, of course; she merely would prefer to delay that moment to when she wore more appropriate clothes.

She spied Lot. Though he no longer served as butler and had been relegated to serving the gentlemen's needs,

Andy reasoned he was nonetheless a servant. She stepped forward to have him summon the twins to her room, but Elysse Farrington sidled up to him first.

There was nothing odd in that, Andy admonished herself. Elysse, having been so lavishly entertained by Reginald Duncan, would naturally turn first to the man's valet if she'd an errand to be run.

But whatever Lady Parsett whispered, Lot did not move when, moments later, the woman hurried away. In that case, Andy thought, he'd be free to see to her own errand.

She made her request. He pretended not to hear. Then again, he might not have heard, she amended charitably, for his mind was clearly intent upon something else.

Tugging on his sleeve, she again relayed her request. With a scowl, he focused on her face. She thought he meant to be rude, but with a curt "Very good, madam," he obviously thought better of it and strolled off toward the twins.

Andy wearily mounted the stairs, cursing her stubborn pride. By lodging with the other chaperons, all she'd proved was that she could climb an inordinate amount of steps. Had she demanded a room nearer her sisters, she would still have breath left to scold them.

It did not help to think of the vast expanse of their lovely room, not when her own was so cramped and airless. Entering it now, she told herself it hardly mattered. She'd spend a fortnight at most in it. The bed was comfortable enough, for all that it was narrow. The sole window might be little more than a slit, but miniatures of her sisters on the battered chest of drawers warmed the room considerably. By adding a few knick-knacks here and there, she could make the place positively cheery.

Yawning, she sat on the bed, ignoring its creaks as she unbuttoned her gown and wondered how best to deal with her sisters. For a weak moment, she wished she need not cope with them alone, that she had a man who could take the burden, just once, from her shoulders. If only Geoff—

Hearing a knock, she nearly jumped off the bed. In her mind she could see Geoff, brought here by his pity and guilt. It took M's breathless "Andy, what's wrong?" to snap her out of such idiocy. As if Geoff would ever climb those stairs for anyone, least of all her.

"Nothing." She jumped up to fling open the door. "I, er, merely wished to speak with you."

"Now?" they said in unison, their breathlessness clearly not a case of worry over her but a result of the climb.

With a forced smile, Andy gestured to the bed, the only seat in the room. Their distaste was almost comical. "It's quite pleasant, actually," she insisted. "Up here with absolutely no one to bother me, I should be able to finish those alterations on your gowns."

They looked so adorably guilty at this, she wanted to kiss them both, but she forced herself to explain her summons. "You do remember why we are here, don't you?"

There was another dual flush of guilt. Satisfied, Andy pressed on. "It was not to make cakes of yourselves over that Boxley and Fallingdown."

"Foxley," said M.

"Bellington," said P with equal indignation.

Andy impatiently waved a hand through the air. "Whatever their names, you are here to win this hunt."

"Oh, but Andy, Fairbright is ever so stern."

"And staid. I never once saw him crack a smile."

Ah, but if you had, Andy thought, before quickly halting herself. "I thought we had agreed you were to defer to my judgment on this."

"Yes, but—"

"Have I given you reason to doubt me? Is there a valid

motive for abandoning months of careful planning? Years of hopes and dreams?"

"No, but—"

"Good." The situation required utter ruthlessness. Their young noblemen were Geoff's friends and could be no more serious-minded than he. For all his quirks, Fairbright was by far the more permanent catch. "In the morning, then, I trust you'll do your best to answer the first question."

"What question?"

"About Fairbright history. You know, the hunt?" The double blankness was more than Andy's tired brain could bear. "What on earth were you doing that you heard none of this?"

"Could it have been when Jamie was telling us about his friend in Vauxhall Gardens? He was . . . well, it was enough to set us off into a fit of giggles."

Andy knew that incident; hadn't she embarrassed herself by unwittingly relating it to the earl? White-faced, she plopped to the bed. She didn't know which shocked her more: P's use of the man's Christian name or her listening to, and then laughing at, such a tale.

"Poor Andy," M crooned at her side. "She looks positively undone."

"So she does." P nodded. "Let's leave her to sleep. There will be time enough to discuss this in the morning."

"Good night, darling," they said in unison, scurrying out the door. "Sweet dreams."

They were halfway down the stairs before Andy realized they'd escaped. She tried to go after them, but the effort seemed beyond her. They were right; she *was* undone. Between the jolting coach trip, the insanity in the kitchens, and the various battles with his lordship, it had been a most tiring day.

And it was but the first.

CHAPTER

7

Staring at the ceiling in the early morning hours, Andy tried hard not to be intrigued by the dowager's hunt, but the twins were right. Of all things, she most dearly loved a puzzle, and this promised to be a prime one.

She caught herself with a stern reminder: She was not here to enjoy herself. She'd come to Fairbright Manor to keep a deathbed promise to her mother. To see the twins wed.

Though given their natures, she conceded with a frown, two weeks might not be nearly long enough to ensnare Fairbright.

In manners and temperament, the twins were peerless, any mother's dream, but not even the most blindly adoring sister could say much for their brains. Information might drift in one ear, but it invariably slipped, unheeded, out the other. Reminding, even hounding them merely led to frustration. Far easier, Andy had long ago learned, to do the thing herself. Sitting up abruptly, she decided that if either twin were to have a chance at success, she simply must find and submit the correct answers for them.

Rising to light a candle—for there was no sense pretending she could sleep now—she groped for her clothes. "Very well, my lord," she muttered as she dressed. "I'll play your ridiculous game for the moment, but only to help the twins." It had nothing to do with her love for a good riddle, she maintained; she was not here to have fun.

As she leaned down for her shoes, she spied a paper on the floor. She lifted it up. It was the first question, apparently slipped under her door during the night. She sat on the bed to read it.

Where can I find the name of the first Earl of Fairbright? she wondered as she slipped into her shoes. The house must have a library, with books describing . . .

Into her mind came the image of his lordship's vast desk, books tumbling across its expanse. It would be as good a place as any to start, though she'd best do so before he woke. The last thing she wanted was for Fairbright to learn of her active participation in his hunt.

Taking no time to consider how the man might react to her rifling through his desk, she hurried down to his study, question clasped to her chest.

Nor did she spare a thought to him as she lit his lamp and pulled up his chair. Engrossed in her task, she set the question on the desk and snatched the nearest book.

It did not describe the family lineage, but curiosity kept her turning the pages. Having kept accounts for the Grange, she saw at once the marked difference between the current earl's stewardship and that of his uncle and cousin before him. It was not solely the nature of the expenditures—theirs were more personal and self-gratifying while his centered on the estate—it was that Richard's invariably led to profit.

There were new tools and vehicles, several key additions to the livestock, and a series of drainage ditches for the fields. Impressed in spite of herself, Andy noted the planned cottages for his tenant farmers. Clearly, my lord had a heart, as well as a good business head.

As this did not fit with her current opinion of the man, she slammed the book shut. Rummaging through the pile, she grabbed another. Not the one she sought either, she grumbled, as it fell open to a carefully etched floor plan.

The intricate pattern of rooms more resembled a maze than any part of the manor she'd seen. Thick black arrows pointed the way to a dark red square at the core. Here, the tiniest of arrows seemed to point downward.

But Andy's attention was arrested by the careful lettering above it. "The original vault of the first Earl of Fairbright," it read, with the name "Alan Duncan" scribbled in a lower corner. Feeling that burst of excitement solving a puzzle always produced, Andy hastily jotted the name of the first earl on her question.

The earl! Slowly, belatedly, she became aware of her surroundings. The enormity of her intrusion sank in at a faster pace. If the man had been displeased about finding her in the kitchen, she thought with a wince, only imagine his reaction to finding her here.

Dropping the book, she went for the door. Behind her, the canary began a maniacal chirping. Having forgotten it was in the room, Andy jumped, half-convinced the earl had arrived to chastise her.

She inhaled deeply to calm herself. Clearly, it was not the earl. Since no bird would squawk so unless deeply in need or desperately in love, and since she found no recipient for the latter emotion, Andy approached the cage.

It was filthy, and as she'd expected, the food cup stood empty. How like the man to neglect his pet, she thought as she reached for the seed, seizing on any excuse to despise him.

Hopping onto her finger, the bird seemed disinclined

to leave. Touched, Andy eased both hand and bird from the cage. The canary perched there, trusting eyes pinned to hers, its tiny head cocked to the side. As she softly stroked its back, she could have sworn it smiled.

"Are you lonely, too?" she crooned as she petted it. "In all this big old rambling house, wouldn't you think one of us could find a friend?"

It was then she chanced to look up to find the Earl of Fairbright watching from the door.

Richard had passed a far from restful night himself. Hardly surprising, what with a houseful of unwanted guests and a most uneasy future. Having suffered through several nightmares in which he'd been pursued by some dreadful female or another, he was in no mood to face any of them today.

Blast his aunt and her brazen stupidity. Bad enough to embroil them in this outrageous house party, but now she must hide a valuable heirloom, the Fairbright emerald no less, somewhere where any ne'er-do-well might stumble upon it. And to make matters worse, she had stubbornly refused to reveal its whereabouts to him. She'd had the insurmountable gall to tell him to follow the clues, like everyone else.

As his rage had yet to cool, and he'd no wish to relieve his anger on some unsuspecting visitor, he'd donned his work clothes. He could at least see to the planting. Since house guests rarely stirred before ten, he should have sufficient time to ride out to the fields and back.

He should have known, however, to except the unexpected from Mrs. Morton.

Staring at her, for he simply could not comprehend what she could be doing here at this hour, he again felt that odd little stab in his chest. How soft and lovely she seemed in the lamp's glow. For what seemed a lifetime, he stood watching the bird, so happy and trusting in her hand, imagining how he would feel in its place.

But then she turned, that scowl and hideous gown transformed her into a crone, and her lonely words became a reproach directed at him. As if it were his fault she was such an antidote.

"And just what," he asked, striding into the room, "are you doing with my bird?"

She drew the thing closer to her chest. "I, why, nothing! It was screeching. Its seed cup was—is—empty."

"So soon?" Irritated, for he'd fed it only yesterday, Richard concluded that if the bird must persist in eating like a blasted lion, someone else must take care of it.

He meant to describe his overburdened schedule, but as he stopped before them, she and the canary huddled in a united front. "I see," he said, irked that she could turn even his bird against him. "Humanitarianism is what brings you to my study at the crack of dawn."

Her gaze went to his desk. Following it, Richard spied a piece of paper and snatched it up. To his disgust, he saw the day's question. That despicable hunt! "The others chose to wait until daylight to start their quest," he snapped.

"I didn't think . . . I thought . . . but you're right. I was wrong to come here without your permission," she said flatly, returning the bird to its cage with a studied lack of speed.

She did not look at him. Uneasily, Richard wondered if she'd cry. Not that a storm of tears could intimidate him; he'd long since achieved immunity under Elysse's monsoons.

He turned his attention to her question, knitting his brows as he did so. What in Hades made her suppose his father was the first Earl of Fairbright?

She snatched it from his hands. "I was likewise wrong to litter your desk, my lord. It won't happen again."

"Your answer is incorrect, you know."

The color had returned to her cheeks, he now noticed, and the militant pose was firmly back in place. "How unsporting, my lord. I thought you wanted me in your hunt."

Richard must have looked as blank as he felt, for she snatched up a book on his desk. "I saw the sketch myself."

So intent was he upon the flashing blue of her eyes, he did not at first take in her words. "Sketch?" he said somewhat abruptly as a result. "What sketch?"

"This one." She shoved it before his face. "It says Alan Duncan, right there!"

Recognizing the book of sketches his father had left him, Richard felt an uncomfortable jolt. He stared at the red square in the center, wondering who on earth could have drawn it there. Having used these plans to finish Alan's maze, he knew it hadn't been on them before.

"This is a plan for the maze," he said absentmindedly. "My father meant to duplicate the original vault, as he was forbidden to work on the original."

"Your father?"

Richard looked up to catch her blushing three shades of pink. At times, he thought reluctantly, she truly could be adorable. "So sorry. Alan Duncan was my father. Many say he did look a great deal like the first earl though, if it's any consolation."

He nodded up at the portrait. Her gaze went from it to him. "I suppose we both share his looks," Richard admitted grudgingly. "But Ross Duncan, as my aunt is so fond of reminding, had the gumption of ten of us. She's right, I suppose. Only pure brass could have convinced Elizabeth to grant him, a Scot straight from the Highlands, the title."

"He must have done her a favor?"

"Several, from all reports, but it was his prowess on the battlefield that won him the earldom. The doubloons, as impressive as they were, could not compare to all this land."

"Doubloons?"

He viewed her sudden interest warily. Was she, after all, merely another fortune hunter? "Tedious business, family history," he said quickly to change the subject. "I had not meant to bore you with it."

She looked at the sketch in her hands. "Actually, I find it fascinating. This Ross built the vault, then?"

"All Scots are somewhat zealous in guarding their goods," Richard replied dryly. "First thing Ross did was to start building his castle. His last deed was in charging his son to carry on his work. It's family tradition, to pass on a dream. From Duncan father to Duncan son."

"As Alan passed on his dream to you?" she asked softly. "That is why you wish to restore the castle?"

Richard could only nod. Staring into those unusual eyes, he grew slowly aware of how disturbingly close to him she stood. Barely a hairbreadth hovered between them; he could feel her warmth as if it reached out to him. Catching a whiff of her floral scent, he inhaled deeply.

Like a doe sensing danger, she grew suddenly alert. Eyes wide and wary now, she too judged the distance between them. She slowly edged backward. "I—I should be going."

Richard said nothing. He did not trust his voice.

"I, er, please forgive my intrusion. I had no right to poke and pry into your private affairs."

She managed to not only place the desk between them, but revive his irritation in the process. "Private, Mrs. Morton? No such privilege exists where my aunt is concerned. She expects you all to poke and pry to your hearts' content."

She bit her lip. "Nonetheless, I—"

"No harm was done," he snapped. "After all, it's not as if you could possibly understand any of this." Exasperated, he gestured to the opened account book.

"No?" She glared at him, not contrite at all but angry

and proud. "I'll have you know, my lord, I kept the accounts for my father's estate."

"I wonder why that doesn't surprise me. Pray tell, Mrs. Morton, is there anything you *cannot* do?"

"I try not to think so."

"Of course. And in your perusal, I trust you found everything in order?"

"Impressively so." The admission was a reluctant one. "It could have been no easy trick, turning this estate to profit again. Your cousin had quite run it to ground."

He refused to react to that, to reveal—or even admit—how her observation pleased him. "My profits are minimal. Not nearly enough to cope with what needs to be done."

He gestured helplessly. How could he explain how tightly his aunt held onto the purse strings, how he labored under a sense of frustration and failure each time he gazed upon the crumbling stone of the castle? "I don't suppose," he blurted out impulsively, "you'd want to help?"

"I beg your pardon?"

"I . . . well . . . the thing of it is, you don't know my aunt. Beneath all she does lies an underlying motive."

The blue eyes narrowed.

"Take this question, for example. On the surface, it might seem innocuous, but I know she knows I keep the volume on family genealogy here. No doubt she envisions me chatting with each of the silly females she's invited here."

"How unreasonable of her."

"The estate is in the midst of an inflexible planting schedule," he explained stiffly. "With all the work to be done, the last thing I want, or need, is some twenty-odd females running and shrieking through my house."

"You could easily have one less if you release me from your hunt."

Confound her eagerness. "No. That is, I need someone to, er, see I am not so harassed. I thought—"

"You thought wrong, my lord." She could not have
been stiffer had a rod been affixed to her spine. "If you
will excuse me, my lord, I happen to be quite busy
myself."

"Wait!" he called after her, adding a far softer
"Please?" If she knew about his aunt's impossible
bargain, about having given his word, surely she would
understand.

She hesitated, which was fortunate, for the door
suddenly swung open. Had she proceeded, it would have
knocked her to the floor.

"Begging your pardon, ma'am. Oh my, and you too,
my lord. I didn't dream . . ." Poor Mary looked almost
comical, twisting her apron in her hands.

"What is it?" Richard seethed with frustration. Since
when had his study become such a thoroughfare?

"We came, me and her ladyship's footmen out there in
the hall, to see to moving your father's likeness to the
drawing room. Her ladyship said you'd toss a fit if we
didn't."

Her ladyship's timing was superb. No doubt she'd be
pleased to learn Mrs. Morton was right now slipping
away. And without his having the slightest chance to
explain. Thoroughly thwarted, he tossed his father's
book of sketches onto his desk. He then noticed Mrs.
Morton's question.

"I say," he blurted out, snatching it up and hurrying to
the door. "You've forgotten this."

She looked at it, and him, quite coldly. "As you so
uncharitably pointed out, it's wrong in any case."

"Perhaps, but I did give you the right answer, and
therefore spared you the odious task of plowing through
dull old family records."

As she reached for the paper, her fingers brushed his.
Richard, once again aware of her proximity, could not

bring himself to release the page. There must be somewhere they could go to talk, he insisted, as he lost
himself in the too-blue eyes.

But the canary screeched violently. His gaze was torn
away to the white kid glove now anchored at his sleeve.
Elysse, fresh and triumphant in pale yellow muslin,
served as a timely reminder of who and where he was.
He swiftly released the paper.

"Unless you wish to find yourself stampeded," Mrs.
Morton said with a curt nod to the glove, "I'd place that
dull old family volume, open to the appropriate page, in
the entrance foyer. I do believe your hunt has begun."

She was out the door before he could blink. The glove
tightened on his arm. Shaking free, Richard turned back
to the cage. Lord spare him, he was in no mood for
Elysse now.

As he tried to quiet the bird, he thought of how easily
it had gone to Mrs. Morton's finger. It had never done so
for its original owner.

"I see you are busy, darling," she purred beside him.
"I do hate to disturb you, but how am I to answer this
question without your clever mind to help me?"

Mary snorted behind them, a sentiment Richard felt
inclined to echo. He thought of Mrs. Morton, alone in
the lamplight, reading his books. Understanding them.
That woman would stand on her nose before she'd ask
for his help.

Misinterpreting his grin, Elysse grabbed his hands.
"Darling, I knew I could depend on you. But let's not
waste time on this silly hunt. Do let's make a day of it,
just you and I. Though we must hurry. The others are
already up and bouncing about the house. If they find
you, we shall never escape."

And how do I escape you? Richard wondered as he
pulled away. He was instantly amazed at the thought. In
the past he'd always sought Elysse's company. Why did

the prospect of spending a day with her now fill him with alarm?

It was that dratted Morton woman, he decided. Waltzing in here, using her audacity to confuse him so badly, he no longer knew what to think or say. What had gotten into him, asking that fortune hunter for help? He'd managed his life in the past without such dubious assistance; he'd continue to do so in the future.

In a spurt of rebellion, he invited Elysse to go riding. Her seductive smile, he told himself, was well worth any delay in the planting.

She went on about how she must change into her habit, but bored already, Richard returned to the book on his desk. Odd, he thought, how someone had marked that sketch.

In a sudden leap, his mind made the connection. His aunt, of course. The old devil; was that where she'd hidden the emerald? He'd bet his boots she'd never expected Mrs. Morton to stumble upon this sketch.

He might have smiled, had he not then glanced up to witness the air of triumph with which Elysse sauntered from the room. His hand tightened on the book. God help him if she were ever to get her hands on it.

Snapping the book shut, he decided he would not miss an important day's work after all. No reason he and Elysse could not ride to the fields. After tromping about in the mud for an hour or two, perhaps she'd think twice before manipulating him again.

Happily acknowledging that he'd grown as devious as his aunt, he slipped the book into his desk and turned the key.

"I say, M, have you seen Andy?"

Her sister looked up from her breakfast in bewilderment. "Why, no. I imagine she's helping Bess bully the servants. Lady Sarah's cook knows nothing of country ways, Bess says, and she's determined to see he learns them."

Sliding into her own chair, Pandora smiled. God pity the poor cook. Though truth to tell, she was selfish enough to be pleased with the arrangement. No one cooked better than Bess Jenkins. Unless one considered their Andy.

"I wonder, P. Do you suppose we should offer our services too?"

"We can't cook." Contentedly eating her eggs, P shook her head. "Besides, we have other work to do. By the time Bellington sees our Andy, he must be half in love already."

"Foxley," M gently corrected, "won't be so easily led. He needs to see her to fall in love."

"Jamie is the same, of course, but we can still provide a bit of a nudge. I've arranged to spend the day with him."

M was clearly shocked. "Dearest P, should you be calling him by his Christian name? And spending the day alone with him? Andy will be livid!"

"Hardly alone, silly girl. We shall make up a party— you, myself, Jamie, Foxley, and Geoff."

"Geoff? Oh, P, after what he did to Andy?"

P shrugged. "Knowing Geoff, I daresay he's unaware she's anywhere near. And until he is, we might as well make use of him. We do need a chaperon of sorts. And we do want to see our sister married, don't we?"

"Well, yes."

"And we want her to marry Bellington, don't we?"

"I suppose."

Odd, P thought much later, that her twin did not correct her with the usual "Foxley."

Bracing her aching back, Andy made her way up the legion of stairs to her room. It was too late now to think of joining the others for dinner. The gay laughter had long since faded.

There had been no choice, however, as Bess had overworked herself into a very bad cold and needed someone to nurse her. As much as Andy might hate to disappoint the twins, she had no desire, nor stamina, to confront that two-faced earl again.

Entering her room, she bristled, as she had all day whenever she thought of him. Imagine his gall, feigning friendship, all to use her as a decoy. Lovely Elysse was to be taken riding, but safe, invisible Andy must stay behind to keep his other guests at bay.

It had been wrong to eavesdrop, and she'd hated herself for it, but better to know the truth. Imagine if she had listened to him. She'd have spent the day listening to Miriam Dennison's braying laughter, while he and his ladylove laughed at her behind her back.

She went to the window, hoping to be revived by the cool night air. She frowned at the tiny aperture. *Just like my life,* she thought. Didn't her future, with its too-few prospects, loom just as narrowly as the view this slit afforded?

Sighing heavily, she gazed out over the estate. Down below, shadowed and mysterious, the maze seemed to brood in the dark. It reminded her of the turning, twisting paths of Alan Duncan's sketch. Just like her life too, she decided morosely; a tangled series of dead ends and detours, a great deal of scrambling about and getting nowhere.

How maudlin she'd become, she scoffed, turning away in disgust, just as a light flickered in the maze.

She turned back, alert and instantly curious. From this distance she could see little more than a faint glow. She thought fleetingly of ghosts, but quickly dismissed the notion. Lady Sarah would never permit them on the grounds.

But what, then? Who could be wandering about at this

hour in a little used part of the gardens? And why? Yet even as she wondered this, the light extinguished. She waited for it to reappear, but the darkness merely deepened.

How bizarre, she thought when she at last left the window. But what a delicious puzzle. First chance tomorrow, she would begin investigating that maze.

But tonight, she realized with a glance at the clock, she had but ten minutes to midnight. Sitting on the bed, she pulled out three pieces of paper to jot down their answers. What was the name the earl had mentioned? Alan Duncan?

No, that was his father. Ross was the name he had so generously given. Coloring, she relived that scene in his study. None of it had been real, of course; certainly not the warmth she'd imagined in his smile. As he'd proved later, he meant merely to use Andy to deflect his aunt's ever-vigilant eye from Elysse. Help him, indeed. If not for fear of his excluding her sisters, she'd tell his lordship what he might do with his hunt.

"Ross Duncan," she wrote, but with her own entry, a gleam grew in her eye. She laughed to herself as she folded the slips. The solution was so simple, only fatigue could have kept her from it this long. Disqualification! All she needed was a single wrong answer. And what better way to defy the earl than by using his own father's name?

That should put paid to his plans of using her, she gloated as she rose and quit the room.

Quickly and quietly, she made her way to the second story landing. A dark blue cloth on the table provided a perfect foil for the gleaming enameled box. Eyes drawn to it, Andy did not notice until too late she was not alone.

The earl wore an idiotic and thoroughly infuriating grin as he pointed out that her slips had no names on them. Refusing to look at him, Andy scribbled in a flustered rush, dropped the slips in the box, and scurried back to her room.

But once in relative safety, she let out a sigh of triumph. *Take that, my lord,* she said with a huff. *Let us see if you can still grin so obnoxiously in the morning.*

CHAPTER

8

The second question was under her door.

Andy had risen fashionably late, confident at having bested the earl at his own game. Optimism buoyed her as she dressed, so much so she almost did not mind wearing the black today. Until she spied the piece of paper on the floor.

Her first reaction was to kick the blasted thing, but she instead stepped past without even a peek. Clearly, there was some mistake. Determined to rectify it at once, she dashed downstairs in search of the earl.

His lordship was not in, she was informed by Grimes, the tall, expressionless gentleman replacing Lot as butler. Would she prefer instead to speak with Lady Sarah?

She would not, of course, for she could not imagine accusing the dowager of making a mistake. Smiling weakly, she told Grimes her problem could wait, and turned rather docilely to mount the stairs.

Two young ladies hurried down them, their eyes red and swollen. "One silly wrong answer and our hopes are done," they sobbed as they shoved out the door.

Andy wanted to chase after them, to offer to take their places, but an uneasy suspicion began to take root. She had submitted an incorrect answer, yet she hadn't been disqualified. Dear heavens, who had?

Taking the stairs in a rush, she envisioned her poor sisters, weeping as disconsolately as that pair now boarding their carriage for London.

It was the earl's fault, she'd try to explain. He'd flustered her so, she'd mixed up the names. The moment he returned, she would go to him, explain, and see things set to rights again.

The apology never left her lips, for the twins were not in their room. Alone there, lifting the scattered piles of clothing, a fully recovered Bess Jenkins gave Andy a dubious glance. "What are you doing here? Thought you were all off to that church."

"Where are the girls?"

Clutching the gowns, Bess gaped at her. "With you, I'd have thought. Off to answer the question."

Again, Andy failed to absorb the woman's words. "I need to explain—to apologize. . . ." But as she paused, their meaning sifted into place. "They are where? Doing what?"

"I told you, answering the question. Skitted off with two pleasant chaps, those lords they've been giggling over."

"They've gone off with Foxley and Bellington alone?"

"I, well, naturally I assumed you'd be with them."

This was said belligerently, as if Bess expected her to shoulder the blame. "You mentioned a church," Andy prodded. "They expected to find the answer there?"

"Seemed so," she huffed as she placed the gowns in the wardrobe. "Hard to tell, the way they giggled."

"Both of them? Bess, are you absolutely certain both twins received a question today?"

"Two questions and two girls. You doubting my eyes?"

"Of course not." Biting her lip, for it was difficult not to doubt *someone's* eyes, Andy decided she must find her sisters. To prevent them from jaunting about unescorted with strangers, of course, but also to learn whom she could have disqualified from the hunt.

She opened her mouth to ask where the church might be, but one glance at Bess stomping about the room with the gowns discouraged this notion. With the woman in such a mood, Andy might better locate the church herself.

Leaving Bess clucking over a torn hem, she hurried to the nearest hall window. From this height, she could see half the countryside. Surely any church worth its salt should have a recognizable steeple.

But once again, all she saw was the maze. It seemed abnormally large in the sunshine, though no less intriguing. Recalling the mysterious light of the evening before, she vowed again to return at first opportunity to investigate.

But first things must come first. She sought another window. This next offered a breathtaking view of the fields, all buzzing with activity. Seeing how many remained unplanted, she began to understand why Fairbright felt inconvenienced by his guests. Though he could consider himself fortunate to have so excellent a foreman, she thought, admiring the speed and eagerness with which the workers obeyed the tall dark man on horseback. . . .

Why, it was the earl, she realized with a start, and working in the same tattered clothes he'd worn that first day on the hill. Clothes he also wore yesterday. Had he been planning to work then, too? Thinking back, she recalled that Lady Parsett had been somewhat irate, and rather muddy, on their return.

Andy checked her smile. She was not here to watch

the earl plant his seeds, however nicely he might sit atop a horse. Proceeding to a third window, she gazed down the winding path to the village. Though she still saw nothing even remotely resembling a church, she decided to follow that route. There would be someone along it, surely, who could point the way.

Midway to the village, she found said someone kneeling in a patch of loosened soil, a forest of potted geraniums spread about him. His lips moved, as if he spoke to each pot as he arranged it.

"Pardon me, but could you—" she began, halting abruptly as she saw the poor man's expression. Andy wondered if he imagined one of the geraniums had spoken back to him.

"I had not meant to interrupt . . ." she tried again.

He rose to his feet with amazing speed and agility for a man of his advanced years. He was not tall, barely an inch above Andy's head, but his cultured tones disguised any lack of stature. If he were an actor, she thought, women would swoon over that voice every night.

"Not at all." His sun-darkened skin crinkled with good humor. "Actually, I was expecting you."

"Me?" Andy looked over her shoulder, certain he must be speaking to someone else. Finding no one there, she decided he must indeed think she was one of his plants.

As he followed her glance to the flowers, he chuckled. "I cut slips every autumn. By spring, I seem to have double the geraniums. My cottage becomes so full of them, I can barely see out the windows. Please forgive me if I now seem frantic about setting them in the ground."

She smiled easily. "My mother had a similar passion. She had geraniums hung from the ceilings with twine."

"Capital idea! I must remember that for next year. Ah, but where are my manners? Would you like some tea, Miss—"

"*Mrs*. Morton. And no, thank you. I am obviously interrupting your work as it is."

"Name's Bellfellow. Cedric Bellfellow. You've come for the answer, I assume?" Her face must have seemed as blank as her brain, for he shook his white head indulgently. "My dear girl, you are here for the hunt, are you not?"

That answer. The one still unread on her bedroom floor. "Oh, no, not I. Actually, I seek my sisters. They are near my size, but, oh, so lovely, with yellow hair and the most adorable dimples. I was told they were on their way to the church. I'd hoped they might have passed this way."

"I fear not, though this would be the path they'd take. I say, do you mind terribly if I plant while we chat?"

"Oh, no, please do. As for my sisters, you might not have seen them, but perhaps you've heard them? They do have this tendency to giggle."

"They sound delightful, but alas, I and my geraniums have been alone all morning. Will you pass me that pot? The red one, yes. Ah, thank you."

"I see. Well, as long as this is the path my sisters must take, and you seem terribly swamped with geraniums, can I help while I wait for them?"

"But your gown."

"It's so old, it can't be damaged. Have you another digging trowel?"

Smiling, he handed her the tool, explaining where each plant should go. "Your patience amazes me," he added with a speculative gleam. "A clever girl like you; why aren't you out winning the hunt?"

"I have no wish to win!" Andy jammed her trowel into the dirt. "Indeed, I've tried to disqualify myself. That's why I must find my sisters. To apologize, you see."

As the poor man obviously did not, she found herself explaining, from the promise to her dying mother, to the

twins' inability to do anything right for themselves. By
the time she'd finished, she had planted four full rows.

"Ah, a most awkward situation," Mr. Bellfellow
commiserated as he began his own fifth row. "Still, in
seeking these answers—for your sisters, of course—you
will need to learn Fairbright history."

"I suppose. But discreetly."

His eyes began to twinkle. "I could tell you a tale or
two. A fascinating clan, the Duncans. As wild as a North
Sea wind. Though unfortunately, that particular trait
leaves too few male survivors."

"Hence, the hunt?"

"Precisely. After Richard, you must realize, the heir is
a distant cousin. Have you met Horatio yet?"

"I don't believe so."

"Trust me, you'd recall. He takes fashion, as he does
all else, to its embarrassing extreme. Not that such lack
of sense isn't common enough these days. Nor even
unforgivable, could he show any sense anywhere else.
The foolish lad has made so many disastrous . . . let
us say 'investments,' Richard's forever in debt trying to
settle his blunt."

"I begin to see why Lady Sarah demands an heir."

"Says she won't abide another weak link in the chain.
Wants another Ross, of course."

"The first earl?"

"None other. A bit of a blade, Ross was, and quite the
devil with the ladies, but he did have gumption."

He had convinced Elizabeth to grant him this land,
Andy remembered. As she envisioned the first earl with
the dark locks and warm eyes of the current one, she
imagined the poor queen must have felt hard put to deny
him anything.

"Oh, yes, Ross was a fighter," that marvelous voice
continued. "But he was also a dreamer. Had to have his
head in the clouds to build Hazard Hall."

"The castle?"

He nodded, then shook his head wistfully. "Chose the site to protect his treasure. Thought the island would make it harder for anyone to steal it away. Unfortunately, it also made it hard for his descendants to live there. Place floods dreadfully, come spring."

"Then why is Ri . . . the current earl so intent upon restoring it?"

"Like Ross, he has his dreams, and dreamers are rarely practical men. Sometimes I think he'd use every last shilling he owns to see that castle restored to its former glory. Though Sarah doesn't help, old hypocrite that she is, by forbidding the work."

The more Andy learned about the dowager, the more confused she became. Sitting on her heels, she studied Mr. Bellfellow, wondering how he could know so much about the family.

"Richard is quite stubborn," he continued, chuckling to himself. "Sarah knows that by forbidding him, you see, she guarantees he will do his best to defy her. Prods him on, she does. Just as she did his father."

Andy burned with curiosity, but it was not at all the thing to go prying for gossip about one's hosts.

Muttering to himself, Mr. Bellfellow grabbed the last geranium. "Can't tell me she didn't leave Barnaby Royce's floor plans out there in plain sight by accident. She knew Alan would snatch them up and use them."

Andy must have looked as bewildered as she felt, for he explained further with a sudden brilliant smile. "Barnaby Royce was the clergyman who helped Ross design his castle. Brilliant man, Alan claimed. But then, Alan was as obsessed with that castle as Richard is."

It's not an obsession, Andy protested silently; *he has a dream to fulfill.*

But when she realized she was actually defending the man, she rose to her feet to change the subject. "My goodness, look at the time. If you will excuse me, I must find the church. My sisters must have used another route."

"My dear, you *are* at the church." He smiled gently and gestured behind her. "You can barely see it through the trees, but all this is church property. The rectory, with all its records, lies but a stone's throw away."

Andy had time enough to take that in, but not all its implications, before he lightly touched her arm. "A dreadful amount of dust has collected on those books," he warned. "Bad for the lungs. Can't you be content in merely being told the answer?"

Perhaps, if she knew the question. "As tempting as your suggestion is, isn't it cheating?"

He chuckled as he stood. "Too true. Not at all the thing for a man of the cloth. *Royce* would be outraged."

Why is he winking at me, Andy had time to wonder, before a deep voice sounded behind her. "Don't let her bam you," the earl sneered. "Cheating is her favorite pastime. Told me herself she'd do anything to win."

Andy had to make a double recovery. If she'd felt foolish learning Mr. Bellfellow was the vicar, she felt a proper clodpole to again be caught prying by the earl. Afraid of what he might have overheard, she snapped, "I told you before, I want nothing to do with your silly hunt."

"Of course not. What is it, twice now you've been the first to the answer?" He turned abruptly to the vicar. "Forgive the intrusion, Uncle Cedric; I'd no idea you had a guest."

Uncle Cedric? What sort of thimble-brain would have confided her life's story not only to the man's clergyman but to his relative as well?

Before she could locate a hole in which to bury herself, they were interrupted again. And the last person she needed to see now, Andy groaned, had to be Lady Parsett.

Elysse meandered up as if out for a Sunday stroll, but

she spoiled the leisurely image by snatching "dear Richard's" arm. In her walking gown of hunter's green trimmed with tiny pink bows, she could have been a vine clinging to his sleeve.

"As you are presently occupied," the earl said to his uncle, "perhaps we can speak this evening?"

"Alas, choir practice is tonight."

"Perhaps tomorrow then? I need to discuss work on the castle."

"Tomorrow?" Elysse tugged on his arm. "Darling, surely you can't have forgotten the masked ball?"

Andy swore she heard the earl groan. The vicar, she noticed, winked at her again. "Mrs. Morton has expressed an interest in *Royce's* castle, Richard. Perhaps you could discuss your work with her?"

"I doubt she's truly interested in discussing a pile of stones."

It was the emphasis on *truly* that irked her most. "Actually, my lord, we had a castle of sorts on the Grange. Nothing quite as grand as yours, I don't doubt, but I do know the value of a good pile of stones."

His smile stretched tight. "I fear mine would merely disappoint you."

"Too true," Elysse gloated. "That drafty old thing should have been dismantled years ago."

Andy watched the earl's face go tighter. Elysse remained oblivious, rambling on about how the stone could be better employed to build a folly. That way, everyone from London would be mad to visit it.

"Our talk can wait," the earl said bluntly, shaking free of his vine. "The ladies are no doubt anxious to be off gathering their answers, and I have work of my own to do."

"Richard, pet, you're not leaving?"

"I must get back to the fields. Care to join me?"

"Beastly man." Elysse gave an involuntary shudder. "You cannot mean to leave me here alone?"

"Alone?" He smiled nastily at Andy. "But here is Mrs. Morton to help you. I hear she wants to make a new friend."

"Of course," Andy said through her teeth. "I'd be delighted to help you, Lady Parsett."

"Splendid. Then I am back to the fields."

"And I shall fetch the key to the rectory," the vicar sputtered, scurrying after him, clearly unwilling to be caught alone with the two females.

"Is this your idea of revenge?" Elysse hissed when the men left, the green making her seem positively serpentine. "Happy to help, indeed. Happy to get in my way, more like."

"I can't imagine what you're trying to say."

"Can't you? That's a needless grudge you've been nursing all these years. I did not take Geoffrey away, you silly child. He fled."

It was Andy's turn to groan.

"One could hope you'd learned your lesson," Elysse continued in a silkier tone. "Can't you see Richard is merely being kind to you? Unless you again plan to make a fool of yourself, do not get in my way where he's concerned."

"You are warning me off? You can't be serious. I could understand such concern over my sisters, but me?"

"The twins?" Elysse gave a throaty chuckle. "Dear, naive Andy. Even had they a prayer with Richard, which of course they do not, they are too busy chasing after Adam and Jamie to take advantage of it. Or didn't you know they went off together this morning? I believe Geoff was along. He hasn't learned, of course, that you are here. Yet."

"Is that a threat?"

Though Elysse still smiled, she did so woodenly. "Go back to hiding in your room, dear girl. Spare yourself the added humiliation."

"Hiding? I don't believe—"

"You can believe this. Were Geoff to stumble upon you now, he would feel nothing but pity." She glanced from Andy's black cotton to her own green muslin. The contrast was vivid. "As does Richard. Dear foolish Andy, go back to your room. Better for everyone if you do."

As Elysse turned to flounce off, Andy couldn't resist a parting shot. "You might do well to follow your own advice. Judging by his lordship's eagerness to return to his fields, it would seem your ploys are as old and worn as my wardrobe."

The woman's glare could freeze a flame. "Make no mistake. Richard and I share a special understanding. You cannot hope to stand in my way."

Holding her perfectly coifed head high, she marched off to wrestle the key from the vicar. She was welcome to it, Andy thought in a snit of her own, for she had no desire to poke amongst the dusty records with a viper like Elysse.

It was not until she had mounted the attic stairs, their height draining her ire somewhat, that she paused to consider the ramifications. M and P might miraculously remain in the hunt, but they'd soon be disqualified without the correct answer.

As if to augment her guilt, the dratted question stared up accusingly from the floor. She cringed as she thought of the twins losing all hope of a marriage, merely because she had twice let her temper get the best of her.

Dispiritedly, she read the question, as she should have done earlier. Slowly, the grin spread across her face. So that was why dear old Vicar Bellfellow had taken such pains to explain Duncan history, why his eyes had twinkled so merrily each time he mentioned Royce's name. Barnaby Royce was the clergyman commissioned to design the original Duncan home, and the answer to today's question.

The smile grew as she wrote it down. She meticulously made certain the twins' slips were correct and that *Alan Duncan* did indeed appear on hers. There must be no confusion, come tomorrow, that she was no longer in this hunt.

"Oh, P, what are we to do? The day has gone by, and we have yet to learn the answer."

"Andy will have seen to it," P hastened to reassure her sister as she helped unbutton M's gown. "She always sees to these things."

"Dear, wonderful Andy. Oh, P, we must find her the very best of husbands, mustn't we?"

P lowered her hands, her expression thoughtful. "You know, I've been giving this a great deal of thought. The more I think on it, the more I see you are right. Foxley *would* be the better match for her."

M whirled, her dress falling unheeded to her waist. "F-Foxley?"

"Indeed. Jamie is too flighty, too unpredictable, for her tastes."

"Oh, but he is such fun, you said. Didn't we agree she deserved to have fun?"

"Foxley can be amusing. Why, remember how he teased you today?"

Her rising color proved M did indeed remember. She looked away, lest her sister remark upon it.

"Good, then it is settled. Together we will make certain Andy becomes the next Lady Foxley."

"Bellington," was her sister's subdued, though no less determined, reply.

CHAPTER
9

A masked ball, Andy thought with contempt. And the third question was a miserable excuse for having it. As if anyone could fail to recognize the earl, even in disguise. No man alive had a smile so . . . so . . ,

She paced across the confines of her room. Perhaps the dowager meant so easy a question as a respite, since a good five carriages had departed for London today. Apparently, these participants had failed to make their way to the vicar.

Andy wished Elysse had been in one of those carriages. It would be awkward facing the woman now, considering what they'd each said. Strange, but Elysse could not yet know the earl's true intent. Else she would never have fashioned the absurd notion Andy posed a threat.

An odd omission on his part. If he'd meant to inspire jealousy, surely he could choose a more convincing candidate? Yet, if he'd meant merely to keep his lady-love forever guessing, then leaving Elysse with Andy yesterday while he skipped back to the fields had been a masterful touch.

As, she had to admit, was the way he kept changing her own answers. Someone must be doing so, else she'd have long since been disqualified, and who else but Fairbright wanted her in the hunt?

He must think me a proper worm, she thought in disgust. The man must feel he could bully her into anything.

And he was not alone. Elysse seemed to think she would happily slither off to spend the fortnight hiding in her room. How absurd of the woman, to fancy Andy would be afraid of facing Geoff.

Then why, asked a tiny voice inside, *haven't you already done so?*

She'd been busy, she protested. There was the kitchen crisis and poor Mrs. Bumfrey's back. With Bess busy running the house again, someone must fashion costumes for the twins.

And what is your excuse tonight, Andy-girl? whispered the voice again.

She was not a coward, she insisted. It was just that she had no real desire to go to some silly masked ball.

She could hear the muffled tunings of a distant orchestra. Unbidden, a wave of longing washed over her. She squelched it at once. She did not want to attend. She was tired, she could not dance, she had no costume. . . .

"Excuses," her father would have scorned. "A true Gratham never retreats."

And as if it were yesterday, and not fifteen years ago, she pictured him tottering on the dining room table as he ripped an ornamental sword from the wall. "Leth them back ya inta a corner," he'd declared, the slurred syllables diminishing his dash, "and ya god no choice but ta come out fighting."

Standing close, ready to catch him though he outweighed her thrice, Andy had absorbed every garbled word.

"And when ya do, see that ya fight like a demmed madman. They'll be so smug, see, thinking they've got you stoppered, you might just take them by surprise."

He'd ended his magnificent soliloquy by lunging with the weapon and tripping over the fruit. Yet from the floor, even on his back, he'd brandished the blade like a buccaneer. "Go down fighting and ya'll never lose. You, Corporal!" he'd commanded, looking her straight in the eye. "Take the sword and finish them off for me."

Ah, Gerry, she thought now with unaccustomed fondness. You were a dreadful father, but never a coward.

It was foolish, and uselessly sentimental, but all at once she missed the silly man. How typical to grieve now, to miss him when it was much too late.

But even could she go to Gerry for advice, she insisted, she'd only get an insult for her pains. Or worse, he'd go charging off like some senseless bull in her defense, just as he'd done with Geoff. . . .

But thinking back, had he truly been so horrible? Why had she never stopped to consider his motive? Gerry's judgment had been clouded by liquor, granted, but he'd meant well. In his typically bullish way, he'd seen only that his Corporal needed her battle fought for her and had proceeded the only way he knew how. Head on.

As now, so must she. She was a Gratham, was she not, the eldest in the line? Without her help, the twins would never uncover the earl's disguise on their own. The man could be wearing a fig leaf and still they would overlook him. And while she might be forced to admit this did not bode well for wedded bliss, she maintained that Fairbright was their sole and final hope; one of them must marry him.

Pursing her lips, she planned her strategy. She would march right up to Geoff, flirt a bit, and take the wind right out of Lady Parsett's sails. She could then further prove her indifference to Elysse's threats by flirting with the earl. Which should also shake his lordship's compla-

cency, she thought in amusement. He might not be so
eager to change her answers if he thought she truly
wished to marry him.

But where do I find a costume? she tried to demur, but
the memory of Gerry, brandishing his blade before her,
would not allow it. Mentally she grabbed that sword, as
she should have done long ago.

She would wear what she wore now. Her courage was
at issue, not her wardrobe. All she need do was waltz
into the room, prove she was undisturbed by Geoff's
presence and disturb Fairbright with her own.

Tonight, Corporal Andrea Gratham would fight her
own battle.

Richard stepped into the ballroom, itching dreadfully
beneath the many layers of padding and face paint. He
had concealed himself behind this particularly distasteful
guise hoping the sight of a wart-faced hunchback would
keep all but the blindest females at bay. He knew what
his aunt was about; he knew her masked ball was merely
another excuse to let these women paw him.

He found himself a quiet corner and a glass of wine.
To his relief, he was left alone. In relative anonymity, he
was free to watch his guests.

Elysse, a predictable Marie Antoinette, played the
social butterfly by fluttering to the door with each new
entrant. Richard chuckled each time she failed to uncover his disguise. Until she mistook him for an over-
weight dragoon proving to be Miriam Dennison, and he
turned away in disgust.

His aunt played a most imperious Elizabeth, with the
rest of the Tribunal posing as ladies-in-waiting. The trio
had outdone themselves, he conceded as he gazed about
the ornately decorated ballroom. A garden of flowers, a
creditable punch, and even the foresight to import extra
male guests for the dancing.

A hooded monk stood beside them. Recognizing his

Uncle Cedric, Richard made a mental note to speak to him later. Partly to discuss work on the castle, but primarily to satisfy his curiosity as to how Mrs. Morton came to be planting his flowers.

He found himself searching the room for her. Two adorable milkmaids, distinctly her sisters, were guarded by a pair of zealous shepherds. Adam and Jamie, of course; not Mrs. Morton at all. She must be hiding again, he decided. Biting her nose to spite his face.

"Richard, old chap, you look ghastly. If I hadn't known you meant to be a hunchback, I'd never have recognized you behind all that face paint. Gads, are those warts?"

He looked up to find a decorous Louis XVI. "Oh, it's you, Geoff."

"You recognized me? I am crushed."

"You look it. But please, lower your voice. I must remain incognito."

Playing with his snuffbox, Geoff stood to the right, pretending to speak to the wall. "Fear not, your secret is safe," he whispered. "Clever stroke, that question. With any luck, you might disqualify every last one of the chits tonight. I doubt there's one with the courage to confront you. Look how they flock to that Henry VIII. Do you suppose they think he's you?"

"Horatio? Lord, spare me, in all that satin and fur? He's atrocious."

"Always is. Oh, my!" As the snuffbox clattered to the floor, an abnormal hush fell upon both Geoff and the rest of the room.

Andrea Morton stood at the door. Though clad in her eternal black, there was something different about her tonight. With a determined air, she sucked in a breath and strode across the room.

"Geoff, here you are," she gushed as she swept up to them. "What have you been about, neglecting me these past few days? Or should I say years? One would think you had forgotten our little flirtation."

"Andy?" was all Geoff said, but it told Richard plenty. Something lingered between them, he thought, something that excluded him. And he found he did not like it one bit.

He began to notice others gravitating closer. He edged backward in his chair.

"How original of you, Andrea. A governess disguise?" Elysse drawled as she approached. "Or is it a housekeeper?"

There was a hesitation so slight, Richard wondered if anyone else noticed. "I would never be so unconventional," she replied, the blue eyes going straight to him. He quickly shut his jaw.

"Andy!" Geoff repeated in a daze. "After all this time, you can recognize me?"

She bent down to retrieve the snuffbox. "Remember, I gave this to you? When I give something away, I never forget."

Taking it from her hands, Geoff turned as red as his rouge. He seemed at a loss for words, a curious affliction for him. What sort of name was Andy? Richard wondered irritably. And why was Geoff permitted to use it?

"How lovely to see you again, Mrs. Morton," Uncle Cedric said to his right. "I see you found the answer, after all."

"I am ever in your debt, Vicar Bellfellow."

As she curtsied prettily, Richard watched her face. Odd that he'd never noticed how clear her skin was, how soft. Or how readily a smile came to those rich, red lips. How the devil, he wondered with another rush of annoyance, had the woman gotten to be so lovely?

"Morton?" Geoff was croaking. "*Mrs*. Morton?"

"I'm widowed now." She would not look at Geoff, Richard noticed. And Geoff could not look away.

"This hunt is the most excitement our village has had," he heard his uncle say.

Jamie, with that ever-present twinkle in his eye, shook his head. "It's not much of a hunt without a treasure. I say we should be searching for the *Duncan doubloons*."

"Doubloons?" asked Mrs. Morton, alert now and far too intent.

"Lord Bellington refers to a legend," Uncle Cedric explained. "Some believe Ross built his castle to protect the booty he earned from Elizabeth, a sizeable collection of Spanish coins. Over the years, countless treasure-seekers have made pests of themselves, digging up the grounds. A nuisance, really, since there is no proof the treasure actually exists."

"Reggie said it did," Jamie bantered back. "And I still think it would make a glorious prize."

Elysse sniffed. "Reggie was a fool. And Richard is prize enough."

"Richard?" Jamie taunted. "Or his title?"

Mrs. Morton, Richard noted uneasily, still watched him. Taking his measure, he'd have said, had she been anyone else.

Ever the diplomat, Uncle Cedric covered the momentary awkwardness by bowing low over Mrs. Morton's hand. "As much as I'd love to keep you young people chatting, I know you'd far rather be dancing. Mrs. Morton?"

"Oh, not me," she demurred. "But I'd imagine Marie Antoinette would adore dancing with her king."

Geoff blinked as if just now awakening. "Uh, yes, but of course. Marie?"

Though Elysse allowed herself to be trotted off, she looked as if the guillotine was too good a fate for Andrea Morton.

As Uncle Cedric led Jamie away, Richard noticed he was now alone with the woman. Her blue eyes focused on his, glittering with determination.

He said the first thing that came to mind. "Don't look to me, Mrs. Morton. I am not about to dance."

"Nor am I, my lord. I thought we might sit and chat."

Trust her to be the only one to recognize him. "How did you know it was me?" he snapped. "You never gave me a thing."

She seemed genuinely surprised he should ask. "Why, I suppose it must have been your smile."

She looked away in embarrassment. Conscious of the many curious ears nearby, Richard asked if she'd mind "chatting" outdoors.

Shrugging, she turned on a heel to lead the way. Once out of earshot, though, she whirled to face him. "You needn't have worried I'd make a scene, you know. I can't dance. I haven't the least idea how to go about it."

She seemed so young in her defiance, Richard relented. "Nor can I, actually," he offered. "Not with this hump. And not without giving myself away. You can't know how unpleasant it is to be fought over so incessantly."

"No, I suppose not, but how unkind of you to notice."

"I hadn't meant to imply . . . oh, drat." Richard felt the customary exasperation rise. "I doubt you accosted me for a mere chat. What is it you want now?"

Even to his own ears, the words seemed impossibly rude. The blue in her eyes went to an absolute frost. "I'm sorry you find yourself accosted so often, my lord. . . ." She paused to take a breath and smile, though the latter was not nearly as gracious as her tone. "But I assure you, I meant merely to do the pretty."

Richard braced himself.

"I wish to beg your forgiveness," she continued. "I should have long since thanked you for your kind invitation."

"The hunt is my aunt's fault, as you well know."

The smile stiffened. "Lady Sarah might have invited

my sisters, but you, kind sir, were the one to include me. I cannot tell you what such an opportunity means."

"Do try."

"When one reaches my age, one becomes accustomed to sitting on the shelf. And while my first reaction was to oppose change, walking about your beautiful estate has since prompted me to reconsider. I see now how marriage could alter my life for the better."

"Just what are you driving at?"

With a coy smile, she placed a hand, à la Elysse, on his sleeve. "You misunderstand me. I've merely taken your advice to heart, my lord. I now believe you were right; participating in your hunt will be great fun."

Leaving him no time to react, if indeed he could have found the words to do so, Mrs. Morton waltzed back into the ballroom.

She was playing a game, he realized. And while he had no idea of her true intent, or even motive, he wouldn't rest until he did. Lord, he thought with grudging admiration, he hadn't battled against such a strategist since Napoleon.

Curious as to what she would do next, he found himself trailing after her. Unfortunately, Elysse and Lot, locked in conversation, blocked the door to the ballroom. Reminiscing over Reggie, Richard supposed, avoiding both by skirting around to another doorway.

Reaching the ballroom, he found Andrea Morton with her sisters, who simultaneously nudged her toward Adam and Jamie. The more she shook her head, the more insistent they became. In the end it was Jamie who stumbled out with her to the dance floor. She had not lied, Richard noticed; she truly could not dance at all.

He watched her count each step, feeling every wince, sharing her profound relief when the ordeal was done. When she was immediately shoved back out, making the same valiant effort with Adam, he fought the urge to go in rescue. She would not thank him, he knew; she'd more likely box his ears.

Having exhausted both gentlemen, she left them with her sisters and fled to his uncle, who bowed and gallantly kissed her hand. Wondering anew about their relationship, Richard edged closer.

By the time he wound through the crowd to reach the unlikely pair, Horatio had joined them. They had gone past introductions and were already embroiled in controversy. As he made his point, his cousin's chest bulged further than normal, even for the Henry VIII costume. "No one wants to wed a bluestocking, madam. A man wants a real woman."

Richard could have warned him, but he was just as happy to see all that frost directed elsewhere.

"On the contrary," Mrs. Morton enunciated. "Men of our class don't want a real woman at all; they want an ornament. A pretty little bauble to hang on a tree."

The sarcasm, delivered in that deceptively soft voice, sailed right over Horatio's balding head. "Precisely! A pretty little thing who knows how to act."

"Oh? And how would we know how? You hire servants to run your house, nannies to raise your children, and a, well, a woman to serve any other need. I ask you, sir, what female with any brain at all wishes to be so useless?"

"My question exactly," Richard said from the shadows. "One might wonder why so many of you are hell-bent upon matrimony."

When she turned to him, flushing a mortifying red, he regretted his words at once. Deep down, he'd agreed with everything she said. What was it about this woman that had him always wishing to provoke her?

She recovered well; he had to grant her that. "Necessity, Lord Fairbright," she said with a brittle laugh. "We girls do love our creature comforts, you know."

"Richard? My good lord, is that you?"

Horatio, in the best of circumstances, did not have a pleasant voice. Nor a quiet one.

"If you will excuse us," Mrs. Morton gloated as a dozen heads snapped in their direction. "I wish to introduce Vicar Bellfellow to my sisters."

All but dragging his uncle away, she left a baffled Richard wondering what the devil was cooking in that brain of hers that she could one moment pursue him like the others and then be twice as skittish in the next.

And if he were confused, poor Horatio, who had just had his first dose of her, looked positively pummeled.

"Kept her father's accounts, you know," Richard mumbled, as if that would explain anything.

"Her sisters are right," Horatio gushed. "She is magnificent." He reinforced this appraisal by scrambling across the room in pursuit.

I will be damned if I'll do the same, Richard swore. Nor could he have. Thanks to Horatio, the female guests who had heretofore ignored him now flocked to his side in droves.

"Forget those doubloons. You are after the emerald."

"You could be overlooking a fortune, madam. More than enough to pay your debts in London."

"Which I would not need, had you made good your promise to bring Reggie up to the mark."

"Count yourself fortunate you did not wed him, for he had less funds than yourself. Do you think he'd have expended so much energy searching for those doubloons else?"

"The man was a fool. If those coins were more than mere legend, Richard would have sought them. I doubt he enjoys toadying up to that decrepit aunt of his any more than I do. Though mark my words, this shall all change when I become Lady Fairbright. Find me that emerald, and Sarah shall dance to *my* tune."

"I am working on it."

"Are you? You are not watching Andrea, as I advised."

"The Morton woman knows less than we."

"Don't underestimate her. She may dress the dowd, but she can be quite clever. Follow her, I say. Of them all, she is the most likely to lead you to the emerald."

Concealed in the shadows, Lady Sarah narrowed her eyes as she eavesdropped on the conversation. Decrepit, was she? They would soon see about that.

She stepped back to a less conspicuous spot, ready to nab Lot the second he hurried past. She did not wait long.

"You, Lot," she said as she skewered him with her cane. "I wish to speak to you."

If she'd startled him, the wretch concealed it well. "I am ever at your service, my lady," he replied, bowing low.

She stifled the urge to poke him again. "It has come to my attention that someone has been prowling about at night," she snapped at him. "You wouldn't know anything about it, would you?"

He never twitched a muscle. "No, my lady."

"As I would hate to bother my nephew with it, I must rely upon you to bring this nocturnal activity to a halt."

"I will do my best, madam."

Of course he would, but not at what she'd asked him. "You have not reported to me of late. Have you not yet learned where my nephew hopes to fix his interest?"

"The hunt has just begun, madam."

In more ways than one, she thought. Wearying of him, she waved a hand. "That will be all."

He left, but the anxiety he'd instilled did not. Contrary to what Richard believed, she did not for a moment trust that Lot. Were there anyone else to use, the man would have long since received the comeuppance he deserved. Not that she feared his implied blackmail, for while he might claim to know some nasty things about Reggie, she knew a great deal worse about him. No, if she kept him on it was because she dared not risk any agent who might confide in Richard. She could ill afford to have them compare notes.

She could control the man, she insisted, but a vast uneasiness wriggled through her insides. For the first time since she'd begun this hunt, she felt unsure of its outcome. God help them all if it did not come about in the end.

In her own chamber, Andy suffered no such qualms. She was quite happy with her evening's work. In all, she rather doubted his lordship would bother to correct her submission tonight.

But to be on the safe side, she'd submitted a correct one. Oh, to see the earl's face as he read it. The poor man would be so confused, if not downright frightened. A few more days of her determined pursuit of him, and he'd be correcting her right answers to wrong ones.

Too restless to sleep, she wandered to the window. She was in such good spirits, the view seemed not nearly as narrow tonight. As she gazed out over the estate, she sucked the cool night air into her lungs, feeling at ease with the world. Until she saw the light in the maze.

She leaned forward, staring until her eyes watered, only to have the light flicker and go immediately out.

Her euphoria died. There was something furtive about that light, as if whoever carried it did not wish to be seen. Was someone hiding there?

Or perhaps they were searching?

Even as she wondered what one might seek, Alan Duncan's sketch of the maze flashed through her mind. So vivid were the words *Duncan Vault*.

Could the emerald be there? Excitement began to bubble up inside her. What a coup it would be, to beat Elysse to solving the riddle of the hunt.

She bolted for the door, stopping as she realized she

would find little in the dark. She'd also need a shovel. Not to mention a good night's rest. To succeed, perhaps her search should wait for the morning.

Though it was not going to be, she admitted ruefully, a very good night for sleep.

CHAPTER
10

Gazing out his bedroom window, Richard cursed soundly. Irksome enough to hobble about as a hunchback at that ridiculous ball; now he must provide an "outing" for the chits his aunt had foisted upon him. In his mind, if the girls were truly as bored as she claimed, she could have found a less obnoxious destination than the maze.

He should be planting his fields, he swore again; not gallivanting through some confounded shrubbery. As the blame must be fixed somewhere, and since his aunt would never shoulder it, he cursed his father for having designed the foolish thing in the first place.

Though he might as well damn himself. No one had held a gun to his head; it had been his decision to waste countless summers seeing to its completion. A tribute to Ross Duncan's defensive genius, his father had called their replica of the vault. Their link to the past.

Unfortunately, it was also a symbol of Richard's frustration. In the end, Reggie had taken credit for the work and installed a plaque with his name at the core.

Bad enough his cousin must commandeer the maze to

search undisturbed for his bogus treasure; now the dowager must make the place a circus? The name on that plaque had nothing to do with locating the emerald. Just like setting the chits to learning his identity the night before, today's question was merely one more way the old shrew meant to torment him.

Working himself into a nice little tirade, he stared across the grounds, but it was not the maze that drew, and held, his attention. It was a slight, dark figure stealthily edging across the lawn.

He recognized her at once—how could he fail with all that black—and he bristled. It was one thing to always be first, but this time her eagerness took her too far. A more civilized woman should at least have paused for breakfast.

His impulse was to call her back. If he must wait for the others, then so must she. But as she hesitated at the entrance, sunlight glinted off the object in her hands. Silenced, he watched her sneak into the maze.

For he could not comprehend, not for the life of him, what the woman meant to do with that shovel.

Andy was wondering the same thing as she leaned on the tool, staring at the dozen towering, twisting paths she could choose. Now that she was actually in the maze, she found she hadn't the least idea where to begin.

Try as she might, she could not recall the details of the sketch. After all, she'd been quite flustered, with his lordship looming so close. . . .

Annoyed at how the memory continued to rattle her, she forced herself to the first path to the right. It came to a halt fifty feet later. A second attempt branched three times before ending as rudely, so she retraced her steps and took a left, but it too went nowhere.

She kept at it, though it was slow going. Once, she thought she heard a muffled giggle, but as the sound was not repeated, she blamed her imagination. Her conscience could not be happy about that stolen shovel, she decided. Then again, the noise could be her stomach growling. She vowed never to skip breakfast again.

She was thinking fondly of buttered scones when she first spied evidence of the nocturnal visitor. Excited, she stared at the indentation where the soil had been freshly dug and hastily—though not completely—reshoveled.

At the next turn, she found another such hole, and then another. Encouraged, she skirted past them. The vault, and therefore the emerald, must lay in the center of the maze. If she could but find it.

Just as she decided to go back, that only a madman could design so many false turns, she tumbled into the core.

She paused, reluctantly awed by the dark, silent hush of the clearing. Rising high above on all four sides, the hedge arched into a ceiling with a four foot opening at the top. Through it, a single ray of sunshine beamed down onto a waist-high marble monument.

She rushed forward, clasping the shovel. It must be a sign from heaven, she decided, proof that it was her destiny to find the ring. With trembling, excited fingers, she touched the gold plaque on the marble. "Reginald Duncan," it read. "The fourteenth Earl of Fairbright."

She hesitated a moment. She felt slightly uneasy, as if someone might be watching. Could the nocturnal visitor be a previous earl's ghost, zealously guarding his vault?

Pooh, she quickly refuted; dead men did not dig holes. She poised the shovel, ready to puncture the soil, when a low, slow drawl sounded behind her.

"Busy at work, Mrs. Morton?"

She whirled about. She might even have hid the shovel, had she the presence of mind to remember it was there. And had she not already dropped the thing on her toe.

"You!" she managed to wheeze. "What are you doing here?"

"Odd," the earl said with a false smile. "I was about to ask the same."

He stepped from the shadows, playing with a cuff as if intolerably bored. Without his buckskins, he seemed every inch the titled gentleman out for a morning stroll. But the buckskins were not all that was missing. Where was Elysse? It was unlike the woman not to be hovering at his side.

Fairbright stared at the shovel. Eyes dropping also, Andy colored profusely. There was nothing else to do but admit in a small voice that she'd been searching.

"I see. Was it necessary to dig so many holes?"

Andy eyed the indentations around them. "I—I wasn't trespassing," she stammered, her guilty conscience getting the best of her tongue. "I—I have as much right as anyone else to follow the clues."

"I'm afraid you've lost me."

"The emerald betrothal ring. It is what this hunt is about, isn't it?"

To her surprise, he threw back his head and laughed. "Ah, Mrs. Morton, I knew you to be eager, but I'd no idea just how industrious you could be. How silly of me to assume you were merely answering the next question."

Andy thought of the question lying on her bedroom floor. She simply must stop this dashing off without reading them.

"Do tell, Mrs. Morton, what brings you to the conclusion the ring is in this maze?"

By this time, Andy wanted to crawl into one of those half-filled holes. "And what makes you conclude that I will stand still while you laugh at me?"

He took a quick step closer, raising a hand as if to detain her, then awkwardly reining it back. "You must understand, Mrs. Morton; my aunt is full of tricks. I cannot begin to fathom what she is about this time, but be advised, she would not want you digging in this . . . this shrine. She considers it my cousin's crowning achievement, you see."

Andy didn't, of course, though she wasn't about to tell him so. Not that it mattered. The earl seemed already lost in the past.

"I spent three long, back-breaking summers completing this maze for my father. It took another to fill in the holes Reggie dug looking for his blasted treasure." With a bitter laugh, he nodded at the plaque. "It was to have read 'From Duncan father to Duncan son.' Trust my cousin to spoil that, too."

"Treasure?"

The earl fixed her with his haughtiest glare. "There was, and is, no treasure. So you see, Mrs. Morton, there's truly no need to be digging these holes."

Andy's sympathy dissolved. The man must think her a nine days' wonder to have dug them all so quickly. Irked, she opened her mouth to mention the prowler.

"You don't go halfway when you have a change of heart," he provoked, changing her train of thought. "Only yesterday, as I recall, you were hiding in your room."

She started to protest that a Gratham would never hide when she recalled she should instead be *showing* him this. Pasting on a smile, she simpered up as she'd so often watched Elysse do. "Oh, but I do so adore emeralds. Don't you think yours will look divine on my hand?"

She raised said hand to show him, only to see how wretchedly work-worn it was. Embarrassed, she tried to pull it back, but he surprised them both by reaching out to grasp it in his own.

It wasn't his masterful, almost proprietary manner that brought her to near insensibility. Nor was it his radiating warmth. No, it was the very rightness of the gesture, the near inevitability of finding her hand in his. She should have worn gloves, she told herself; she must never go out without them again.

Yanking free, she edged backward, keeping the wretched hand from sight. She half expected it to glow, or some other silly such thing.

"So you like emeralds?" he pressed, closing the distance between them.

"No. Yes. That is . . ." She realized she was babbling. She should be intimidating *him*, not backing into the marble. *Pay no attention to how tall he is*, she warned herself. *Or how nicely built*.

But he was there, so near and overwhelming. And he was staring quite rudely at her lips.

Flustered, she blurted out the first thing to come into her head. "You cannot mean to kiss me?"

His lips, at which she was likewise staring, curved into a grin. "And why not?"

Deny him, she thought desperately. *Protect yourself*. "I—I heard giggles. Others might see us. Do you wish to be forced into offering for me?"

He leaned closer yet, mere inches away. "Come now, Mrs. Morton. Surely others have tasted those sweet lips without resorting to matrimony."

How could Geoff tell him? Stung by a sense of betrayal, she forgot to back away.

His voice was little more than a whisper, a caress of a sound so close to her ears. "My dear, any good flirt knows a kiss is not a declaration."

All she could see were lips, so firm and full, and so near above her. "N-no?"

"No indeed. It is a trifle, a thing of pleasure. It means nothing." His eyes focused on her mouth, which had gone suddenly dry. One inch more and they would touch. "Shall I show you?"

Without waiting for an answer, which would have taken a great deal of time to formulate, he took her in his arms. It was a soft motion, as if he feared breaking her, yet not one bit indecisive. And like the clasp of his hand, it seemed the most natural thing in the world.

She slid into those arms too readily, her lips going to his with unerring speed. All the longings, frozen inside, came achingly to life, and Andy began melting from the inside out.

As his arms tightened, folding her close, she happily relinquished her last scrap of pride. It could have been no other way.

Her hands had gone to his neck, to the soft, fascinating curls at his collar, when with a low moan the earl pulled abruptly free. They stood there for what seemed the longest time. She, dazed; he, glaring.

"You see," he spat out at last. "There truly is nothing to it at all."

He could have struck her. Nothing at all? Determined not to crumble before his eyes, she turned on a heel to flee.

But she had forgotten his shadow. Elysse blocked the exit, those well-plucked brows raised the slightest inch.

"I was showing Mrs. Morton the plaque," the earl said belligerently.

The brow rose a bit more, but Andy, too busy putting distance between them, did not remain to see it. *He kissed me,* she thought frantically, *and I wish I had died.*

Hurrying back along the paths, she wanted nothing better than to hide in that horrid room for the rest of her life.

But the day was filled with nasty surprises. Just as she neared the exit, Horatio's portly form emerged to block her way. He beamed with delight.

"Ah, Mrs. Morton, your sisters told me I might find you here. Is this not a lovely day to stroll through the gardens? How fortuitous that we are alone in the maze. Come, shall I escort you to the core?"

As he grabbed for her arm, Andy stepped backward.

In her alarm, she had forgotten about those unfilled holes.

Even before she hit the ground, Horatio was there to lend his hand. She found herself being yanked up, into his chest, before she could even regain her breath.

"Mrs. Morton . . . Andrea . . . are you all right?" he huffed in her ear, his grasp tightening painfully. "Forgive me, but you are so soft, so lovely. . . ."

Horrified, Andy realized he too meant to kiss her. It was then, of course, that Richard and Elysse happened along. Andy began to push at Horatio, but it was too late. She already looked as guilty as sin.

Elysse could not have been more pleased. "We should go, Richard," she said so anyone in the house could hear. "We seem to be interrupting a tryst."

"What do you think you are doing?"

Horatio seemed to shrink under his cousin's blatant rage. "B-but, Richard," he sputtered. "Y-you don't understand. It isn't as it appears."

"Is that so?" Richard scowled so fiercely, Andy feared his eyes might pierce her skin. Indeed, her chest ached so, it felt as though they already had.

"I fell," she tried, but her voice faded off under that withering glare.

"I am aware of your distaste for conventionality, Mrs. Morton, but I could have hoped you might set a better example for your sisters."

He nodded behind her. Andy turned to see the twins. Beside them, grinning from ear to ear, stood Geoffrey Stone.

She felt the heat of embarrassment, but it swiftly warmed to anger. How dare Richard take her to task where anyone could hear, for something he had so recently attempted himself. "You can't expect me to feel penitent, my lord," she told him coldly. "Not after the example you set for me."

This time, he was the one to look as if he'd been

struck, and he reacted just as Andy had, by turning and stomping away. Elysse, naturally, went after him.

"Richard was ever the boor," Horatio whined, again snatching at her arm. "Now that he's become the earl, he's unbearable. I marvel at how Aunt Sarah endures him. If the courts would but let me assume control, Fairbright Manor would be a far different place, I can tell you."

"Would it indeed?" It was too much; Andy simply could not abide any more. Pulling free, she snapped at him. "You ingrate. What of the loans your 'unbearable' cousin has provided? His castle could be restored by now had you not plunged him further in debt. You should be ashamed of yourself, saying such things about him."

Horatio's face went white; the poor man looked as if a favorite pet had bitten him. Dear me, Andy sighed as he too marched off. That outburst had cost her her one and only suitor.

"Two down and only me to go," Geoff chuckled at her side. "I must say, Andy, you certainly haven't lost your bite. What sort of a setdown have you in store for me?"

He was teasing, she knew, and on any other day she might have fallen into the spirit by taunting back. But not today. Not after that devastating kiss. "Just leave me alone," she cried, running for the house.

In her haste to escape, she failed to see the wistful, and perhaps considering, expression on Geoff's face.

The twins, however, did not.

CHAPTER

11

"Oh, P, do you think we truly ought?" M glanced uncertainly from her sister to Geoff, and then to lords Foxley and Bellington, waiting on horseback behind them.

P clearly suffered no such misgivings. "You heard Geoff. Andy needs a day of rest. We can learn how the Duncan doubloons vanished ourselves. Let's prove we are perfectly capable of answering today's question."

M could not pull her gaze from Lord Foxley. Spending the day with him would be sheer heaven. She and P had been so busy pushing Andy at Geoff, several days had passed with no more than a quick greeting from him. A sore temptation. But also an abominably selfish thing to consider.

"Andy's been dreading this jaunt, you know," Geoff drawled. "Says she hasn't a proper habit, or some other such nonsense. Though I imagine it's Horatio she hopes to avoid."

She followed his amused gaze. Overwhelming this morning in pumpkin-colored riding attire, the earl's cousin perched atop his horse, eyes darting about anxiously. Amazing, he should continue to seek Andy, considering how blatantly she discouraged his suit. M sighed. They'd made a dreadful mistake there, and now she and P must somehow divert Horatio's interest elsewhere. Matchmaking, like deception, could indeed weave a tangled web.

"Besides," Geoff went on, "you know how she sneers whenever you mention the treasure. Do not fret over her. I will see she enjoys the day to the utmost."

M wondered why she hesitated. Leaving Andy alone with Geoff, especially at his instigation, was all they'd worked for and more. And heaven knew the outing would be well-chaperoned; all eight remaining contestants, as well as Miriam Dennison's shrewish mother, would be tagging along.

She looked back to Adam. With a delicious thrill, M saw he did not wait upon the odious Elysse but was instead smiling at *her*. That was the crux of it, of course. Wanting this time with him so desperately, she very much feared Andy's welfare was not her primary concern.

"Go on, the pair of you, go learn what happened to those doubloons." Geoff grinned toward his two friends. "And don't you dare return without the answer."

Jumping on her mount, P needed no further coaxing. M, unfortunately, still felt the bite of guilt. "But, Geoff, Andy will be ever so miffed if we leave her behind."

"Leave her to me. I daresay I can still manage her. As I recall, all I need do is make her laugh."

How true, M realized. It had been quite a different Andy in those long-gone days when Geoff came to call. If P was right, and their sister merely needed fun, wasn't he just the one to supply it?

So she was not being selfish, not really, in going off with Adam. If their goal was to bring him up to scratch, Geoff's fatuous grin proved how near they were to

achieving it. Vital, she thought, he now be alone with
Andy. But that would never occur until they dragged the
tenacious Horatio away.

She mounted with a dazzling smile. There could be no
sin in relishing this time with Adam. Not when their
dear, precious Andy would herself have such a wonderful day.

An assessment not readily shared by her elder sister.
As Andy glanced about the empty dining hall, she was
nearly as miffed as M had feared. Having snatched
Terese's finest muslin morning gown, something she'd
vowed never to do, and having wasted the better part of
an hour in donning it, she found nary a soul to appreciate
the effort.

Sheer vanity, she fumed, turning back into the hall.
However well the powder blue might match her eyes, the
dainty cap sleeves and delicate lace did not befit a female
of her years and situation. The black had suited her well
enough; she should have remained content to wear it.

After all, who had she hoped to impress? It was not as
if she cared a twig what the earl thought of her
appearance. She was relieved—yes, relieved—that he'd
avoided her of late. Let Lady Markton suffer his boorish
attentions. If Andy felt a trifle put out this morning, it
was merely because she had missed the opportunity to
tell him so.

Indeed, if she'd dressed for anyone, it had been for
Geoff, in appreciation of his aid these past few days. If
she now knew Hazard Hall was so named for the dangers
posed by constant flooding, that Henry Duncan had
therefore built the Manor, she must thank sweet, amusing Geoff for helping to find the answers. His lordship
certainly hadn't helped discover how the first earl had
distinguished himself against the Armada, or how Elizabeth had then rewarded him with the doubloons. In-

deed, if one listened to Richard's snide remarks, she'd think the treasure never existed at all.

She pulled at her half-gloves, fighting a resurging anger. What a despicably confusing man. Treating her by day as though she were bubonic, yet continuing to change her answers each night. Using her, while despising her, yet taking her into his arms in the maze . . .

She softly touched her lips. By all that made sense, how could they still tingle so alarmingly? Geoff's kiss had never affected her so.

For a weak moment, she stared at the bonnet in her hands. Perhaps if Richard could see her in such a pretty, feminine thing . . .

She scowled, then stomped out of the house. She would not think of that man a moment more. A second more. She was here solely for the twins, she must remember, the twins. . . .

Hearing their giggles, she halted in midstride, a soft smile slowly replacing the scowl. Bless their hearts; she should have known her sisters would never abandon her.

Though she must not test their patience. Quickly donning the bonnet, she hurried to join them. But when she rounded the corner, they were riding off with the annoyingly persistent Foxley and Bellington.

Determined to give those two rogues a piece of her mind, she stormed into the stable to demand a mount. The groom merely gaped.

"I am Andrea Gratham," she snapped. "Er, Morton. A—a guest. I need a horse."

He was too well trained to say "Dressed like that?" but Andy knew he thought it. "Not to ride," she impatiently amended. "To attach to a conveyance."

He shook his head, saying there was not much left to offer, as the other guests had removed all but the straw. There remained only Lady Sarah's carriage, an ancient farm cart, and that plow horse there.

Andy stifled a groan. The closed carriage required a

minimum of five coachmen; the cart would barely seat her. With its touch-me-not stare, the nag proved less encouraging. If its back sagged further, its belly would touch the ground.

"But it must be gentle," Andy tried hopefully. The groom shook his head again. Had the temperament of a mule, he warned, and the friendliness of a snake.

Not to be daunted, for her sisters were out with those Lotharios, Andy demanded the horse be hitched to the cart.

Scratching his head, the groom did so. Five minutes later, no less dubious, he presented the reins. Andy took them, squarely facing both his doubt and the nag's glare. She'd driven a hundred carts in her life, and a good portion of her father's cattle had been in a sorrier state than this.

Still, it took several attempts—the last aided by the groom's slap to the mare's flank—for the animal to budge, and then, it was at best a plodding motion. Andy groaned, certain it would take hours to get to the door.

But with the irrationality for which her sex was often unfairly tagged, the mare bolted and charged for the lane. "I forgot to tell you!" the groom shouted behind them. "She likes the wind in her ears!"

Andy barely heard, preoccupied with preventing too much of said wind from entering her own ears, as the bonnet had long since been consigned to the stable straw. Yet the more she sawed on the reins, the more the nag took umbrage. With the devil himself glinting in its eyes, it dashed down the lane.

Andy hoped only to remain within the cart. For all her experience with horses, this one surpassed comprehension. Even as she gained control, or thought she had, the nag stopped in its tracks. The cart, which in all justice should have slammed into its hind quarters, instead veered sharply to the right, pitching both itself, and Andy, into the mud.

On paper, she had applauded the earl for building his ditches, but sitting in its oozing mess, she no longer considered drainage desirable at all. The cart was mired a good six inches and sinking steadily. The nag was trotting happily down the lane.

When I catch up with it, Andy swore, *I will give it a good deal more than wind in its ears.*

Blessedly, the nag had not traveled far. It stood around the bend, placidly munching grass as if the treat were its due. Nothing in its stance, Andy noticed with absolute loathing, revealed it had the slightest intention to move.

She wasted the better part of an hour coaxing, tugging, and shoving the wretched beast. For every inch gained, she lost a yard of composure. She was fit to burst when she at last led the beast to the cart.

As she tried to explain what must be done, it fixed her with an unblinking stare, much like Lot did. Recognizing that pleading was a waste of time, she tied its reins to a nearby tree and began freeing the cart herself.

It had seemed so small in the stable, but here, lodged in the mud, the cart assumed mammoth proportions. Heaving with all her weight, she inched it up the bank. Yet as she gained the edge, her abused muscles gave way, letting the cart slip back into the ditch. It sent up a spray of malodorous mud, building on the previous layer already staining Terese's lovely muslin gown.

She pleaded over her shoulder, hating herself for it. Particularly when the mare continued to chew. Grabbing the cart again, she hauled it halfway up the bank. She was indulging in a most unladylike—though gratifying—string of oaths when she glanced up at a grinning Fairbright.

In utter dismay, she released her hold. The cart slid with a vulgar sound into the ditch between them. There was another insulting spray of mud.

It's not fair, was all she could think. To spend all that time on her toilette, only to face him in all this muck?

"See what comes of always needing to be first, Mrs. Morton?" he said nastily, using his handkerchief to wipe the splats from his face.

"First?" she sputtered. "What monumental conceit. You and your hunt have to be the last thing on my mind."

It was a splendid setdown, and would have served well, had she not slipped, sliding with undue speed into the mud.

The earl, blast him to perdition, barely contained his mirth. Taking care to cover his hand with the handkerchief, he leaned down to offer his aid.

It was dreadful, unforgivable really, but faced with his laughter, she could do no less. One quick tug, and his lordship toppled into the ditch with her.

Though not in the way she'd envisioned. A great deal of lost pride had gone into that tug, and a heapful of anger. She landed beneath him, with his long, taut form sprawled atop her, his warmth seeping down into her body. A warmth that increased as she remembered their kiss in the maze.

Against her will, her gaze traveled upward to the brown eyes, now dark and thunderous. *I've gone and done it,* she groaned. *I'll be lucky if the man doesn't flay me alive.*

Flaying had to be the last thing on Richard's mind. He too was remembering that kiss, and wondering why, if it truly meant nothing, he was so tempted to try it again.

"I am so sorry," she said abruptly. "I—I don't know what came over me."

Richard, who'd been wondering if he dare dab the splats from *her* soft skin, heard the "over me" and scrambled up. He felt every bit as boorish and clumsy as his cousin Horatio. A Fairbright, he should have remembered, did not go about entertaining his guests in a ditch.

He offered a hand, belatedly recalling what the gesture had cost him earlier. Something flickered in her eyes.

With a reluctant grin, he helped her up. "Spare us both an apology, Mrs. Morton. We know I deserve being brought so low."

A tiny grin twitched at the corners of her mouth. "I'd have thought you'd be livid."

"Do you truly think me such an ogre? No, pray, do not answer." Richard unconsciously moved closer. "The guilt *is* mine, though. I should never have teased you so."

"I should not have reacted so violently. Nor would I have, I hope you realize, if not for that wretched nag."

Richard followed her narrowed gaze to the mare. Having had his own experiences with Old Sal, he began to chuckle. "What's she done now?"

"Your beastly horse stopped. The cart didn't."

"You weren't badly hurt, I trust?"

"Nothing was bruised. Aside from my dignity."

Trying not to chuckle, Richard reached for his handkerchief. "Here, let me see if I can . . . oh, drat, this cloth is muddier than you."

Her eyes went impossibly wide. Too late, Richard realized his fingers were gently wiping away the mud. And that they were in no real hurry to finish the job.

Worse, they were making their way to her lips. Lips he sorely needed to touch. To kiss. Mesmerized by the sight of them, he leaned down, ever so slowly. . . .

She pulled away. Color staining her mud-freed cheeks, she turned with stiff shoulders to climb out of the ditch. Richard, feeling more like Horatio than ever, followed.

"There's not much sense in freeing that cart," he said sharply as he reached dry ground. "Ride my horse, and I will take, er, lead old Sal."

She looked at her gown, not at him. "Can you imagine

the talk were I to gallop into your stables without a sidesaddle? And wearing all this mud?"

"For pity's sake, Mrs. Morton, I had not thought you to be so missish."

"I, missish?" Her voice went so high, he thought it might squeak. "If anything, my lord, it's your sensibil-ities I protect. You are the one forever harping upon my unladylike behavior."

"My dear woman, I never harp. I asked merely for decorum. You answer me with defiance."

"Defi . . . why, you hypocrite, do *you* mean to claim decorum, after the way you behaved in the maze?"

Richard scowled, reliving the distaste he'd felt at finding her in his cousin's arms. She hadn't been screeching then; could she actually prefer Horatio's touch to his own?

To lend credence to this, she spun that moment on a heel to hike off down the lane.

Richard shook his head, still feeling the softness of her skin on his hands. He couldn't understand, not for the life of him, how so tender a moment could erupt into such a nasty scene.

Slapping the horses' flanks to send them home, he, too, turned to the lane. Up ahead, Mrs. Morton's spine seemed so stiff, any good wind could make it snap. He was a fool, he readily acknowledged, as he nonetheless hurried after her.

"Weather's a bit off," he said inanely when he reached her side.

She did not reply.

"It, er, might even rain tomorrow." He paused to open the gate to the drive, glad of the brief opportunity to study her face. Too brief, for as he secured the gate behind them, she again scurried off.

He grabbed for her arm. "Please, don't run off," he said in a rush.

"I don't run away, and I do not hide," she said with

undue vigor. "Can't anyone understand I prefer to be alone?"

Richard dropped the hand, not so much because of her waspish attack as for the distress he sensed behind it. "I understand fully," he tried to reassure, "having trouble with privacy myself. Still, I'd hoped, er, thought, you might need a restorative. My study door is right here before us."

"A—a restorative?"

"Brandy can do wonders to ward off a chill."

"I know what a restorative does," she snapped, but a good deal of the bite had left her bark.

"Then can I tempt you? I promise not to keep you a moment longer than you wish." He opened his study door, hoping she'd follow. It was her health that concerned him, he insisted; it compelled the invitation. Yet his pulse made an unwarranted leap as he felt her presence behind him.

"I say, is that your canary making all that noise?"

"Hungry again," he muttered as he held aside the drapes, annoyed that he must share this time with the bird. "I wish there were someone I could trust to take proper care of it."

"Poor thing." True to his fears, she went straight to the cage. "You're not hungry at all. You're lonely, aren't you? Stuck here all day, there's nothing to do but eat."

Scowling again, Richard went for the brandy. As if she knew a thing about loneliness. Why, the way Geoff leaped to her beck and call of late . . .

Not that it was any of his affair. Ruthlessly pouring, he managed to splash brandy over his desk. As he began to mop it up, he noticed the state of disarray.

He now detected a lingering scent in the room. Elysse? That, clearly, was why the bird was screeching, but what the devil could the woman possibly want on his desk?

His mind leapt backward, to the book he'd secured

there. Unnerved, he unlocked the drawer. To his relief, the book of sketches remained where he'd left it. Untouched.

He picked it up, glancing over to find Mrs. Morton watching him. Setting the book down, he grabbed the glasses. As he set the brandy beside her, he remembered how she had once crept into his study without permission. The bird never objected to *her* intrusion. Had he given the canary to her, he'd wager, she would not have left it to starve. One could trust a woman like Andrea Morton, he realized with a start. Thank the stars she alone knew about that sketch.

"I—I want to explain," she started, playing with the bird. "What happened with . . . between your cousin and me, that day in the maze, wasn't defiance. I did nothing to encourage him to act as he did. I fell, you see, and . . ."

She frowned, still not looking at him as she set the bird back in the cage. "It was a mere misunderstanding, of course. But not one of *my* making."

This inspired a feeling of such relief, he both drained and refilled his glass without knowing he did so. You could trust a woman like Andrea Morton, his brain kept repeating.

She placed the bird in the cage, carefully closing the door as she turned to watch him.

"Forgive me if I implied anything, er, improper between you," he said impulsively. "You were quite right, you know, in calling me an ogre. I have not been myself since this blasted hunt began."

He went to his desk, snatching up the sketches. "Do you remember that first day we met, up on the hill? You said you could not fathom how anyone could subject himself to it. Well, I want you to know. This is why."

He handed the book to her. She seemed confused, but no more so than himself. Was he truly about to put his future into those well-formed hands? "I'd never have agreed if I didn't so desperately need the money," he rushed on. "You saw the accounts. To restore the castle according to my father's visions, I must have the bribe my aunt has offered."

She looked up from the book. Richard did not realize he'd been holding his breath until he saw the understanding, even compassion, in her eyes. He let himself breathe. "I know I must sound a proper mercenary, but those walls cannot withstand the onslaught of another winter storm."

"Perhaps if you should look for those doubloons—"

"There is no treasure!" he barked, miffed that she could throw that accursed myth in his face now. "Confound my aunt. She knows full well those doubloons vanished when Henry tried to move them here from the vault. Check the court records; Anson Fyfe stole and no doubt spent every one. If you still have doubts, look around you. Don't you think if a fortune existed, I'd have long since found it and put it to use?"

As Andrea blinked, obviously startled, he spoke more gently. "It's just another of her games. She's prodding us all toward something. I only wish I knew what it is."

"Can't you refuse to play along?"

"I fear not. I've given my word, you see."

She half smiled. "The word of a Fairbright? Geoff tells me it is not an oath to be taken lightly."

Geoff again? Just how often, he wondered irritably, had they been discussing him? "Quite so. My word is sacrosanct. Still, I have not lived all these years with my aunt for nothing. To paraphrase, I will cheat, not to be netted."

She had the good grace to blush. "I know."

"You know?"

"That you've used me to thwart your aunt. Among other things." She blushed again, then hurried on. "I quite understand, truly. In your place, I'd have done the same."

"I—I must be free to choose my own bride," he asserted, feeling he'd somehow lost control of the conversation.

"I know."

Of course she did; the infuriating female always seemed two steps ahead of him. "What I am trying to say," he said in his haughtiest Earl-of-Fairbright tone, "is that I am happy to pay for your aid. I'd offer the family betrothal ring, given your penchant for emeralds, if not for its present significance. Perhaps another gem will do?"

She did not move. She can't want that gaudy bauble, he hoped. Or was it emeralds in the plural she sought?

With a heavy sigh, she plopped into his favorite chair. "I don't want your gems," she said flatly. "I have behaved abominably enough to deserve so low an opinion, but all I've truly ever wanted is to see my sisters wed."

"My dear Mrs. Morton—"

"But there you have it. I am not Mrs. Morton: I am Miss *Gratham*. I never had a husband. I dreamed him up."

"There is no Mr. Morton?" Odd, how that pleased him.

Biting her lip, she nodded. "The word of a Gratham is no less binding, my lord." Then, in a torrent, she explained her vow to her mother and the increasingly difficult task of fulfilling it. "So you see, I must see the twins wed," she swore as she wound down.

He shook his head. Another female would find a husband first and deal with her sisters later. Intent upon keeping her word, Andrea had overlooked her own future, her own happiness. Richard winced, realizing how he'd misjudged her. And how badly he'd managed things from the start.

"Forgive me," he said softly. "In lieu of a monetary bribe, what say I offer my aid with your sisters?"

"You? How?"

Unflattering, that skepticism, yet deserved. "A season in London should do the trick, with me as sponsor. Between my recently elevated position and my aunt's expertise and connections, we can guarantee the twins entry into the highest heights of the haute ton."

"I see. And for this *aid*, just precisely what is it you expect from me?"

"Nothing dire. Only that you win the hunt."

"And then refuse you, of course."

"Well, yes." Strangely enough, he found himself wishing she had not said that.

"I must say, you show remarkable faith in my abilities." She stood, her smile strained. "But then, should I fail, you need only change my answer. As you did last night."

"Last night? Why, I never . . ." Richard blustered. He might have changed one or two at the start, yes, but after the ball, when she'd turned so aggressive, he hadn't been certain he wanted her in the hunt.

"If not you, my lord, then pray tell who did? I do not deceive myself that anyone else wants me in the hunt."

A good question, and one to set a less dazed mind to thinking. "I never touched it," Richard repeated stupidly.

With a shrug, she moved to the door. His father's book was in her hands.

"Wait," he called out.

Though she paused, she did not turn to face him. "I shall endeavor to win your wretched hunt, my lord. Rest assured, you will be free to choose the woman you love."

Richard had raised a hand to call her back—for the book, he insisted—when Geoff appeared in the doorway.

"Andy, here you are! I've been searching this age and more. Where have you been?"

"Don't ask."

"You can't have found this mud here. Oh, my, you didn't sit in Richard's favorite chair? And drinking his brandy? Good heavens, girl, he's likely to murder you."

Richard began to protest that it was quite all right, that he'd invited her in, when Geoff swooped the girl into his arms, the book of sketches falling unheeded to the floor. Richard was rendered as speechless as she.

"As ever, I must come to your rescue. Though I must say, Andy-girl, you look quite done in. Took a fall, did you? Never could stay atop a horse."

To Richard's astonishment, she giggled. "Put me down, you charming idiot. I'm staining your new cravat."

"Are you? I shall see its repair is deducted from your allowance. Where did you say your rooms were?"

"Top floor. What a prince you are to carry me there."

"I quite see your point. If I let you go, then, you'll swear to hurry back? You promised to show me the maze, remember."

They wandered off, bickering playfully. *How easily she laughed with him,* Richard thought, a vivid contrast to the stilted conversations they seemed doomed always to share. Lifting up the book of sketches, he wished she could at least have remembered to bid him good day.

He would put a stop to such antics in his house, he decided, letting his resentment boil. Geoff would be warned that such familiarity, such lack of decorum, would not be tolerated here, however dotingly Andrea might smile upon it.

What could possibly linger between them? he wondered with an uncomfortable pang.

His hand tightened on his glass. Before the night was done, he would know what it was.

CHAPTER

12

Dear Geoff, Andy sighed, settling back into the window seat to draw the cork from the brandy. How like him to have a restorative sent to her room—without a glass. Giggling, she raised the bottle to her lips.

It was not nearly the first time she did so.

Sobering somewhat at this realization, she lowered the bottle. Ladies, she well knew, did not drink brandy. Though why she would worry, she did not know. Richard would persist in branding her a hoyden no matter what she did.

Besides, it was a comforting beverage, brandy. Helped ward off the chill of this drafty alcove; helped her forget her earlier conversation with him. Or, at least, it should.

It would be just like him to have such ineffective liquor at hand simply to keep her memory clear. Those words about choosing his bride had been a warning, as direct as his sense of courtesy would allow, that Andy must not take his proposal seriously. As Geoff had explained, Richard's choice was, and always would be, Elysse.

Yawning, she stared out the window, trying to discern the outlines of the poor man's castle in the dark. One day, he'd come to realize Elysse did not share his father's dream, that she'd provide little aid for his endeavors, but by then it would be too late. Perhaps Andy *should* hold him to his marriage offer, for his own good. At least she knew better than to waste his pile of stones on a folly.

Stifling another yawn, she set the bottle on the sill and hugged her knees to her chest. How weary she felt. And sad. Here was the earl, adoring Elysse, while she saw only his wealth and position. And there was Horatio, his devotion wasted as Andy squandered her sighs on a man with impossible dreams. There was neither justice nor sense in love.

Annoyed, she stretched the hem of her dressing gown over her chilled toes. She was cold and lonely. Since spying on another was just the sort of adventure he delighted in, she should have asked Geoff to join her. She could picture him, jumping through the drapes with an *"Aha!"* as he caught Richard in the act of changing her wrong answer to a right one.

Dear Geoff, she repeated, stunned to find nothing the least romantic in her appraisal. All these years of mooning over him, only to discover in this drafty alcove what he must have seen long ago. She'd always be too headstrong for his easygoing nature. Even with all the fun they shared, they could never make a go at marriage.

She still should have asked him along, she repeated stubbornly, knowing deep down she was glad she had not. Brandy loosened one's tongue, after all, and no one must ever know the true reason she watched that box.

Not, she sniffed, that she didn't have an altogether practical reason for learning if the earl lied to her. Imagine if she trusted him, if she won his hunt and thereby excluded the twins, only to learn too late he'd no intention of honoring their bargain? Blind faith was all well and good, but not if unwarranted, and not if it cost her sisters a suitable match. That, she insisted, was her sole reason for waiting in this uncomfortable place.

It had nothing to do with the endearing sincerity she thought she'd seen in his eyes. Or the hope that he . . .

She was too weary for this. Laying her head on her knees, she felt the world spin. Geoff was right; she *was* done in. With a lopsided grin, she doubted he would ever again send her brandy—not once he'd seen the job she'd made of that bottle. She should get up now and hide the evidence.

But her head refused to budge. Overwhelmed by another yawn, she granted herself a few minutes' rest. She would just close her eyes for a second. The box was on the other side of the curtain; she'd hear anyone who'd come to change her answer. Plenty of time to rise then.

But her knees made a perfect cradle, and her eyes were so heavy . . .

It would be some time before she again opened them.

"Cigar?"

True to Richard's hopes, Geoff snatched at one. Beside him, Horatio gulped down his port, tidied his chartreuse satin waistcoat and announced it time to join the ladies. Cigar smoke, as Richard well knew, turned his cousin's features a shade to match his clothes.

Since for them, *ladies* clearly meant the Gratham twins, Foxley and Bellington bounded after him. Richard rose to fetch his finest cognac, dousing all but the three closest candles. With just he and Geoff in this cave of a dining room, he needed to create a more intimate atmosphere. Sitting, he poured a generous amount for himself before holding the bottle questioningly over his friend's glass.

"Spanish cigars and French brandy?" Geoff chuckled as he raised his glass to be filled. "What's this, a bribe?"

"From me?" Richard forced a laugh. Of all times for Geoff to be perceptive. Nor did it help that the fire hissed

and crackled behind them as if laughing at his ploys.
"It's been too long a time since we've sat and talked, you
know."

"Too true." Geoff blew out a huge, aromatic puff of
smoke. "That's what we get for letting a woman come
before friendship. All that time wasted, spatting over
Elysse."

"I suppose love makes fools of us all."

"Love?" Geoff leaned back in his chair, drawing on
the cigar. "My dear man, we were a randy pair of young
bucks, sniffing after the first skirt to tempt us."

"You always did have a vulgar turn."

"But I am right, and you well know it. What we felt
for Elysse was lust, pure and simple."

"Granted. But it could happen again. We could desire
the same woman, with neither willing to give way," he
said, leaning over to refill Geoff's glass. "What then?"

"We are gentlemen, Dickie my boy. Brawling over a
female simply is not good ton."

"I daresay you are right." Refilling his glass, Richard
swallowed the brandy with his impatience. This next
question must seem casual. "But what if we were in
love?"

Geoff eyed him through the haze of smoke. "What is
this, waxing sentimental? Must be the goose livers. I did
warn they would disagree with you."

"No, not sentimental. Merely practical. In one week's
time I must offer for one of these women, don't forget.
I already risk a battle with Adam and Jamie should one
of the twins be the victor. If your feelings are likewise
engaged, I would hate to damage our friendship again."

"Lud, man, relax. I outgrew Elysse years ago."

"Perhaps, but what of Andrea?"

Geoff was visibly stunned. He sat upright, cigar
forgotten as he blurted out, "Do you mean *my* Andrea?
Andy?"

Irked, for Richard did not consider her Geoff's at all,

he snapped, "What an absurd name. *Andy,* for heaven's sake."

"Blame Gerry, not me. Claimed his wife betrayed him by producing a girl, so he punished her by calling the child Andy. She retaliated by giving him five more daughters."

"All like Mrs. . . . er, Andrea?"

Geoff shook his head. "Andy? Lud, no. She's one of a kind. Gerry raised her to think and act like the son he wanted. Was wont to call her Corporal, as I recall."

That explained a great deal, Richard thought. "Must have made it difficult to find her a husband." He tightened his grip on his glass. "I don't suppose you and she, well, ever came to an understanding?"

"You mean marriage?" Geoff relaxed back into the chair. "Certain things were assumed, for we were quite in each other's pockets in those days, but I ask you, matrimony? You know me, my friend. I seek fun; not a wife."

Richard leaned back to savor his drink. Nothing quite so satisfying as good cognac.

"Though thinking back . . ." Geoff stared dreamily at the smoke curling above his head. "Being with Andy always could make me laugh."

He smiled a secret smile. Richard began to drink more ruthlessly.

"She's not like other females, you know. Took control of the Grange at fifteen. Did a rum job of managing it, too. Got to be a habit with her, though, this managing."

Richard pounced. "That's why you chose Elysse instead?"

"Me? As if I'd the chance to choose. Andy dragged me outside to prove I belonged to her. Should have discouraged her, I suppose, but she can be singularly determined. And in truth"—he paused to grin—"it was not an altogether terrible experience. At least not until Gerry caught us at it."

"I must be dense. How did you then go off with Elysse?"

"Well, she appeared at my elbow, implying I'd already offered for her and warning me not to fall in the Grathams' cleverly laid trap." He sighed wistfully. "Should have known better, of course. Gerry was too skunked to be clever, and Andy, well, is too bloody proud. Should have seen the starch in her shoulders as she faced the laughter from that crowd. She never once crumpled, except perhaps in the eyes. All these years later, I can still see the hurt in them."

A hurt that remained, Richard thought uncomfortably. He'd seen it often, seen it staring out when her guard was down.

"The worst ten seconds of my life," Geoff continued, "was seeing Andy stroll into your drawing room last week. Though I should have remembered what a sport she can be. Girl never could hold a grudge."

Richard reached for the bottle. It was empty.

Unaware of this catastrophe, Geoff went on. "You know, talking with you has brought the past into focus. It's set me thinking. With you making the lunge, and Adam and Jamie inches from the parson's trap, perhaps I've been a bit of a laggard. A man could do worse than Andy Gratham, you know."

"But she is so deuced unpredictable," Richard blurted out. "One can never know what the woman might do next."

"Well, I say. Just because you don't like her—"

"I never said I didn't like her. It's just, well, look at how deeply she has involved herself in this hunt. I fear she's gotten into that flighty head of hers that becoming Lady Fairbright might be what she wants."

"Rest easy." Geoff chuckled. "She's just here for the twins. Has great ambition for her sisters, you know."

Too well. "Still, she could win. What then?"

"You are more than safe, man. Wouldn't have you if

you were the last man on earth. Finds you . . . how did she say it . . . ah, yes, an arrogant, manipulative bully."

"Oh? And just how does she find you?"

"I am working on that, my friend." Geoff took a long, irritating draw on the cigar. "I am indeed working on it."

I need more brandy, Richard thought irritably. He knew better than to blame the livers for this ugly taste in his mouth. It was the highly unpalatable fact that he'd learned more than he'd wanted to know.

He stole a glance at his friend complacently smoking his cigar. Geoff had every right to feel smug. Undoubtedly knew he could break the poor girl's heart a dozen times and still she'd forgive him.

But not me, Richard surprised himself by thinking. If Geoff hurt her again, he'd pop him good and proper.

"Poor Richard. Livers still troubling you?" Geoff suddenly rose to his feet. "Need me to fetch one of Mrs. Bumfrey's remedies?"

He shook his head sharply, resenting his friend's concern. Couldn't Geoff see another female had somehow managed to wedge her way between them?

"Why not just retire for the evening?" Geoff went on. "I can make your apologies to the ladies."

Richard nearly forgot his resentment in the face of this temptation. Play along, and there would be no need for small talk, no listening to Miriam Dennison pound out her painful tunes, no being grabbed by the nearest available female. "I'd be grateful," he answered quickly. "Though I daresay I shall be all to rights in the morning."

"Indeed you shall. I've never known your housekeeper's remedy to fail."

Geoff went, leaving Richard no chance to deny a need for any concoction. He left the room awkwardly silent, as well, letting too many unbidden thoughts rush in in his wake.

Richard rose to pace the room. Thought him an arrogant, manipulative bully, did she? Wouldn't have him if he were the last man on earth? Why, he wondered with mounting vexation, hadn't she told Geoff about *his* kiss?

Could it have meant so little to her? But that had been the objective, hadn't it? To prove he could kiss her silly and they would neither of them feel a thing. And proved it he had. Conclusively. Only why, then, had he come so close to repeating the lesson today?

Damn the woman. Worming her way in here, disrupting his well-ordered life, driving a wedge into an otherwise stable relationship. Not this time, Richard vowed. Rather than risk Geoff's friendship, he would get rid of her. Get her out of his house and out of his life.

Storming from the dining room, he took the stairs two at a time. Accuse him of changing her answer, would she? Well, this time, he'd change it to a wrong one. Come morning, she would be out in the drive.

He did not stop to think how irrationally he might be acting—or how much the brandy might be contributing to his actions. He knew only that he wanted peace and quiet in his life once again. Sanity.

He never reached the enameled box, for as he neared the top of the stairs, he heard giggles. Having no wish to be seen, especially by her sisters, he ducked into the curtained alcove. Seconds later, they appeared at the table.

"Did you hear that?"

Richard froze, praying they could not see his shoes beneath the drapes.

"Oh, M, do stop fretting. Mrs. Dennison will make certain the others are engrossed in Miriam's performance. Amazing, how one girl can murder a tune."

"Do hurry, P. Someone might yet escape."

Unlikely, he knew; not with Agatha Dennison standing guard. Curious now, he peeked through a slit in the curtain.

Pandora Gratham was shaking her head as she scribbled. "Tsk, M. One would think this the first time we changed Andy's answer. You should be quite relaxed about it by now."

"But it's so terribly dishonest. Only think if we were caught."

Her mission clearly done, Pandora turned to face her sister. From the back, Richard thought, she looked rather like Andrea in her determination.

"Just consider Andy's fate should we not change it. Without her here, how can we set Geoff in her path? We can hardly get them together alone if Andy is on her way back to London. And you do want him to propose, don't you?"

"Yes, of course. But you know Andy. She might get so involved in the game, she'll win the hunt. What if, due to our meddling, the wrong man offers for her?"

"She can always refuse him. Much tidier, actually, for then neither of us need fear becoming Lady Fairbright."

"Oh."

Oh, indeed. Clever maxim, that one about eavesdropping: one never did overhear good things about oneself.

"Pinch your cheeks," Pandora was admonishing her sister. "You need color in them before we can join the others."

Richard was watching them amble off and wondering how to foil their plan when he first heard the sound. It was just the faintest noise, barely a whisper, coming from behind him. He whirled, his mind tripping through the entire gamut of horrors, from his aunt to a long-forgotten Fairbright ghost, but by now he should have known to expect Andrea Morton.

Head propped on her knees, arms hugging herself for warmth, she made a most forlorn figure. He tried to maintain his wrath, summoning up every grievance against her, but his heart softened in a most betraying fashion. Silly puss, why was she sleeping here?

But he knew. She had come hoping to catch him changing her answer. To prove that he had lied to her, that he was no more trustworthy than any of the other men in her life.

Amazing, how much the thought hurt. Especially in light of how very nearly he had proven her right.

She stirred then, ever so slightly, disturbing something on the window seat beside her. Snatching the bottle before it could fall, Richard smiled indulgently. Not his best brandy, but it would nonetheless provide warmth. Poor girl. Half a bottle; hers must have been quite some vigil.

Setting the bottle to the side, he wondered what to do. Her embarrassment would be fierce, and woe to the fool who woke her. Still, she'd likely freeze to death if left here. Perhaps he should fetch a blanket?

As she stirred again, her knees buckled, causing her head to loll. Without thinking, Richard grabbed for her, thinking only to protect her from harm. As he swept her into his arms, hairpins tinkled to the floor.

Her honeyed hair spilled over his hands in a soft, luxuriant cloud. The urge to protect her swiftly deepened into much, much more.

She cuddled into his chest, and his heart contracted. "Ah, Andrea," he heard himself whisper into her hair. "If only you could trust me."

Foolish, to have spoken aloud. If she should wake now, there was no logical way to explain what she was doing in his arms. Or where he thought he was taking her.

If his insides had been unsettled before, they were now in utter chaos. He wished he were half the cad she branded him, for he could then give into this impulse, march to his room, and lock the door behind them. But she lay so trustingly in his arms, and he turned instead for the stairs.

Gazing down, he tightened his grasp. Having her in his arms this afternoon, how could Geoff so easily let her go? Richard would climb a legion of stairs before he'd willingly do so. A lifetime of them.

The skirt of her dressing gown slipped, revealing a soft white ankle. Richard hesitated, then made up his mind. Rather than risk stumbling into someone, a person less than discreet, he would place her in an empty room along this hallway. At the rate his aunt was disqualifying the chits, one must be unoccupied.

Three stood empty. He chose the blue for its superior furnishings, as the color matched her eyes, though it did, coincidentally, lie but a few doors down from his own.

He hurried to the four-poster bed, but when it came time to deposit his charge, she sighed and snuggled deeper into his chest. How easy to forget all but the warmth of her body, he thought in a daze as his grasp tightened. Far harder to turn now and walk away. She looked so lovely, hair fanning across his arms. Just a few minutes more, he pleaded with himself. What could be the harm in that?

"I say, Richard, I thought you were not feeling quite up to snuff." Brow raised high, Geoff stepped up to place a foul-smelling liquid on the bedside stand. "Won't be needing this remedy after all, I see. I say, is that *Andy*?"

Richard would have given his last shilling to be invisible. "It's not as you think. I can explain—"

"You insufferable cad." Even in his cups, Geoff played the outraged suitor to perfection. "Give her to me at once."

Richard stepped back, clasping her tighter to his chest. "Quiet, ox; do you wish to wake her?"

"Better to ask, what do *you* wish to do to her?"

As Geoff stepped closer, Richard realized how absurd

they were. Arguing like boys, they would soon have her up and screaming at them both. It might be wiser to set Andrea in the bed so they might continue this in the hall.

Having done so, he grabbed Geoff's arm and dragged him to the door. "Poor thing's dead to the world," he tried casually. "Found her asleep in the hall, you know. Thought it best to disturb her as little as possible."

"We can't leave her like that," Geoff protested, plainly as loathe to leave her. "Not in her dressing gown."

"What do you suggest? That we undress her?"

Geoff looked shocked, but whether by the suggestion or belligerence behind it, Richard preferred not to know. "Of course not," Geoff countered. "You should fetch her abigail to do the necessaries."

"She has an abigail? Where?"

"Down cozing with Mrs. Bumfrey. Daresay Bess Jenkins will be up in a flash, once she knows *why* you summon her."

Richard now remembered the temporary housekeeper and their brief exchange. Geoff was right, she should tend to Andrea, but he had no intention of summoning her himself. "If you know the woman, you get her," he told Geoff. "Can you imagine the talk if I roused my staff at this hour? For Andrea's sake, this must be handled discreetly."

"Fine time to think of that now." Geoff glanced back at the sleeping form on the bed. "You should be ashamed of yourself, forcing yourself on the poor girl."

"I did nothing of the kind!"

"Must have. Ain't like Andy to swoon."

"She didn't faint, for heaven's sake; she merely fell asleep." He nudged Geoff into the hall. "Which is your fault, I wouldn't doubt. You've had her scurrying about the estate all day. And laughing all night, from what I hear."

Geoff could afford to grin. "She'll be livid when she

learns you carried her, you know. Better drink that remedy. If you think your stomach bothers you now, wait till morning when she's rung her peel over you."

Would she be so angry? It seemed impossible, the way she'd snuggled into his chest. Of course, he realized with a pang, she could have been dreaming of someone else.

"You know," Geoff offered, "it might be wise to say *I* carried her. Since she's known me for absolute ages, she won't be nearly as miffed then."

"I can fight my own battles, thank you."

"But why would you wish to?" Geoff patted him on the back. "No, you just leave Andy to me, my friend. I know best how to deal with her."

And with that, Geoff sauntered off down the hall. Staring after him, Richard was far from reassured. Why indeed would he wish to involve himself? Had he any brains, he would march this instant to his room.

But he did not. Instead, he found himself again at Andrea's bedside, wondering what it was about this woman that would not let him go.

A thousand images filled his brain. He saw her in his kitchen, so proud as she presented his dinner. Smiling over the accounts in his study. Pale and shaken in the maze, after their kiss.

And through it all, each time he touched her, she had been thinking and dreaming of his good friend Geoff.

So be it. Resigned, ready to accept this, he reached for the counterpane. Geoff's was too valued a friendship to risk for just any woman.

It took but one glimpse at her delicate face to acknowledge that this was not just *any* woman. Andrea Gratham was one in a million. Hands tightening on the counterpane, he conceded he wanted her. Badly. Bluster and rage and deny it all he might choose, he would always want her.

The recognition was as inescapable as it was inevitable. If only he could have accepted it that first day on the hill. Instead of alienating her at every turn, he should have been telling her she was the one woman he could ever love.

For it was too late now. With her precious Geoff saying the very same words, nothing Richard could ever say would do the slightest bit of good.

Gently, so slowly as not to waken her, he drew the counterpane up over her shoulders. "I love you, Andrea Gratham," he let himself whisper into her ear.

Then, touching her cheek just once, he sighed and left the room.

He did not hear, in his hurry to be away, Lot's soft chuckle behind him.

CHAPTER
13

Forcing one eye open, Andy peered through the dark. Her entire body throbbed, and her mouth felt as dry as straw. Spying a glass on the bedside stand, she groped for it and forced herself to swallow.

She wished she had not, for the foul concoction was enough to make her gag. Her head spun so, she shut her lids, only to fall within seconds into the comforting oblivion of sleep.

"Glad to see you're awake," Lady Sarah boomed at her elbow. "Been waiting this hour and more for you."

Andy bolted up, eyes widening considerably. Sunlight now streamed in through pretty white-lace curtains. She could not even whimper, dumb as she was with astonishment, for no matter how often she blinked, the walls remained a pale, pleasant blue. This was not her cubicle. That much was plain, though little else was.

Regal in a neck-high, silver-gray morning gown, the dowager perched on a chair beside the bed. Her gnarled fingers tightened upon her cane. "Out with it, girl," she barked. "What was my nephew doing in this room last night?"

"Nephew? Th-the earl?"

"Only one I have." Supporting her hands on the cane, Lady Sarah raised her chin. "When I said Fairbright needs an heir, you know, I meant a legitimate one."

Muddled Andy might be, but not even the village idiot could miss such an implication. Her only confusion stemmed from *why* Lady Sarah uttered it.

"What was he doing here?" the dowager demanded again. "Speak up. I abhor ditherers."

"Uh, why, nothing. Apart from a few words at dinner, I did not even see the earl last night."

"You show a low opinion of my intelligence, girl."

"On the contrary," Andy returned, irked beyond courtesy now. "You have the low opinion. Anyone even remotely connected with the earl knows he is first and foremost a gentleman. The idea that he . . . with me . . . it's preposterous!"

"No man is immune to a pretty woman's wiles."

Torn between gaping and laughing in her face, Andy blurted out, "You actually fear your nephew might be tempted by *me*?"

The cane banged like a gavel on the floor. "Richard was *seen*!"

"Impossible, I tell you. I fell asleep on the window seat and I . . ." Struck by a sudden, hazy memory of strong arms around her, Andy flushed from the inside out. How the devil *had* she gotten into this room?

"Just how are you proceeding with the hunt?" Smiling secretively, Lady Sarah veered off in another direction. "Got any idea where the emerald is yet?"

"Almost," Andy was forced to lie. "A clue or two more should do the trick."

"Think yourself clever, do you? Did you think to get a jump on the others yesterday by riding off on your own?"

Andy colored, remembering all too well the result of

that ride. But no doubt the dowager knew about that, too.

"Fyfe swore he never touched them, you know."

Anson Fyfe was the one who'd stolen the doubloons, Richard had told her. But what was Lady Sarah trying to say?

"Damned fool Henry," the woman ranted. "Should have left the gold in the castle vault where it belonged. He was such a pathetic miser, I'd not put it past him to steal the doubloons himself. And then blame his poor overseer with the theft. Question is, though, where would he hide them?"

Andy, ever prone to a good puzzle, excitedly pondered this. If she could find the treasure, Richard would have more than enough to restore Hazard Hall. Then he'd have no need to continue his aunt's farce of a hunt.

"Useless introspection," the dowager said, rising abruptly. "Don't you be going off with the others to the castle, girl. Spend the day in bed. You've clearly been overdoing things."

"In bed?"

"I can't have you sleeping in my halls."

"Nor winning your hunt," Andy countered. "I know you want me out of the competition. You want Miss Dennison to win. Though I doubt his lordship will be pleased by this."

"The boy knows his duty." Head high, the dowager hobbled to the door. "Richard will do what must be done."

"Even if it makes him miserable?" Andy pressed, leaning forward in the bed. "Is that what you want for him?"

With a half-turn, Lady Sarah pinned her with a rock-hard gaze. "One might as easily ask what it is *you* wish for him."

"I—I—"

Waving a bony hand, the dowager continued out the

door. "What you or I wish is irrelevant. Fairbright needs an heir, and Richard must see to it. It is as simple as that."

The cane tapped off down the hall. *As simple as that,* it seemed to echo, leaving Andy to wonder why, if it were so simple, the future now seemed so complicated. Daunting question, that. What indeed did Andy want for him?

She refused to consider it. Hopping from the bed to dress, she bumped into the bedstand, tilting the empty glass there. Puzzled, half remembering, she sniffed at its rim. She recognized the remedy; she'd fed it often enough to her father. She should thank whoever had left it, for she felt quite remarkably well, considering—

The bottle, she thought in sudden panic; she'd left it in the hall. The hall she never remembered leaving. How on earth had she gotten in this room?

She whirled, now noticing her belongings neatly arranged about her. Everything was in view, from hairbrushes to the miniatures of her sisters. Two black gowns hung in the wardrobe, as well as Terese's few remaining unaltered ones. Reaching for one, she thought frantically as she dressed. Someone had done a thorough job of moving her. But who?

There was a snippet of memory, so vague she could have dreamed it, yet so warm and wonderful she prayed she had not. Her fingers paused, dress half-buttoned. It was the barest sensation, no more than a scent. But *his* scent, framed by a whispered word or two as his lips brushed against her ear.

Flustered hands worked at the buttons. It meant little, she insisted. Richard would do as much for any female so lacking in taste as to render herself senseless in his hall. There was nothing the least remarkable . . .

The memory lengthened. Her fingers went to her lips. Whoever had set her upon that bed had done so with a gentle kiss. And whispered words of love.

Like an echo, something fluttered behind her. She whirled to find the canary flapping its wings. She stood for the longest moment, simply staring, before she began slowly to move toward the cage. He'd wanted someone he could trust with its care, he'd said.

Delight burgeoned. Of all the people in the house, she was the one he chose.

There was a rude, jolting knock. Hastily pinning up her hair, she rushed to the door, but it was only the twins. They spilled past into the room, adorable in their cotton frocks, pink for P and mauve for M. "Hurry," they said in tandem. "Geoff wants to be off."

"Geoff again?" Andy blurted out, irked not to find Richard there. "How many times must I tell you not to involve yourselves in his mad schemes?"

"I am wounded." Looking anything but—indeed he seemed in the pinkest of health—Geoff lounged in the doorway. "I have sacrificed my day to you, and you brand me a scoundrel?"

"It's the question," piped M.

"Geoff is here to help," added P, tugging M back out into the hall.

Altogether too pleased with himself, Geoff scooped up the paper under the door. It was indisputably her question, one more in a long line she should not have received.

So Richard *had* lied to her. All along, he'd meant to change her answer. He'd only moved her into this room to keep from being caught in the act.

Lips pressed together, she grabbed for the slip. Geoff held it beyond her reach. "What say you girls?" he teased. "After abusing my reputation, doesn't Andy owe me a ransom?"

But the twins had already slipped away. She could hear them chattering down the hall, and from the way they giggled, she knew they must have found Foxley and Bellington.

She started after them, but Geoff blocked the doorway. "I must say, you look uncommonly lovely this morning."

Stunned, for the man had never before paid a compliment, Andy whirled to view herself in the mirror. She barely recognized herself in the soft yellow cambric, with its scooped neckline and tight-fitting sleeves. *There is a matching reticule somewhere,* she thought, fighting a growing sense of disorientation. *I really should find it.*

"Particularly when one compares your appearance to, say, last night?"

Andy, having gone to the wardrobe to look for the reticule, turned back to face him. "You saw me last night?"

"I should say so. I moved you."

"You?" No, her foolish heart protested; please no. "But why?"

"Silly chit, could I leave you snoring in the hall?"

So much for whispered words of love.

Silly, to feel such disappointment, she tried to tell herself. She should be relieved. Especially if she had snored.

"And my things?" she said aloud when the silence stretched too long. "You moved them as well?"

"All but the woodwork. I must say, I thought you'd be pleased. You needn't sound so dismayed."

"But it is not like you to go to such trouble." Andy gestured feebly about her, trying to make him deny it. "My clothes, my pictures? Everything?"

"Uh, well, Bess saw to the work, but I insisted you be brought nearer to the other guests. And *me.*"

Ignoring that, she went back to her search. "And the bird?" she asked over her shoulder. "Was it your idea too?"

"What bird?"

So Richard had done that much. Not out of trust, though, she must realize. The canary had become a

burden. Leaving it in her care was no more than the act
of a desperate man.

"Never mind," she snapped as she found the reticule.
"It doesn't signify in any case."

"My, but we are dour this morning," Geoff drawled
behind her. "Goose livers disagree with you, too? But
no, I see you drank the remedy I brought. Must be the
weather, then. Dark skies make for dark dispositions,
they say."

Irked that he'd left nothing for Richard to have done,
Andy turned to tell him to leave, only to find him
looming over her. "What are you doing here?" she
gasped. "Should anyone see you, there will be no end to
the talk."

" 'Tis me, Geoff," he soothed, taking her in his arms.
"Besides, who's to see? The rest, what's left of them, are
all off to the castle."

An expedition, Andy now recalled, from which the
dowager had tried to discourage her. "I don't suppose,"
she said, pulling free to go to the door, "you know how
to reach Hazard Hall?"

He stared at her as if she'd proposed a trip to the
moon. "That relic? My dear girl, you can have no idea
what getting to that island entails. I ask you, how can we
have a romantic interlude in a rowboat?"

This was proving to be a most extraordinary morning.
First Lady Sarah, and now Geoff, spouting off nonsen-
sities with such conviction. Had the entire world gone
mad?

As if to prove that it indeed had, he came up behind
her again and pulled her close to his chest. "Do let's find
a secluded spot instead, to resume where we left off.
Before Elysse came between us."

Andy gaped at him. *If he kisses me*, she thought in a
panic, *I just know I will laugh.*

She pulled away firmly. "I want to visit the castle.
Will you join me, or do I go alone?"

"You're serious?" He tilted his head, hands yet extended. "Of all the madcap adventures. Look at your gown, for Lud's sake. It is hardly suited to such an expedition."

"If you will not help, I shall row the boat myself."

"But I hate the sea, and you know it. What if we capsized? I might drown; I don't know how to swim."

"I do." She left the room, confident he would follow. "If you fall in, I shall save you."

"Heartless wench. You are that determined?"

One thing was certain; she was not about to spend the day in bed. Lady Sarah obviously hoped to hide something from her, something Andy was all the more bent upon finding. If she had to swim there, she was going to Hazard Hall to uncover every last one of its secrets.

Richard climbed the stairs in remarkably good spirits. Irksome, to be upbraided by his aunt for an indiscretion he had not committed nor could ever to hope to commit, but at least he now knew what must be done. Andrea would not suffer for his behavior. Thanks to that meddlesome Lot and his aunt's ensuing lecture, he now had an excuse to offer her marriage.

He paused, thinking uneasily of how the dowager had smirked through the interview. Something was hatching in that devious brain, something his actions abetted. He wished he'd the foggiest notion of what it could be.

He shrugged, more concerned with how to make his offer. Words of love and tender gestures were useless; Andrea would only laugh in his face. Nor could he threaten, though she must be made aware of how badly she needed the protection of his name to save her from social ruin.

But why would she believe him? With all the brandy she'd consumed, she might not remember a thing. Brightening, he stepped back into the alcove, remembering a certain brandy bottle there.

Lifting it up, he saw her again dozing on this window seat. He did this for her sake, he insisted. Someone must keep the little hoyden from harm.

It was then that he heard her voice. Something swelled in his chest, only to shrivel at Geoff's reply. So much for friendship, he thought angrily. In his haste to get there before him, Geoff must have camped outside her door.

He listened to him claim to have carried her. Richard held his breath, waiting for the proposal he'd meant to make, but Geoff spoke instead of romantic interludes. He was so relieved, he had the brandy uncorked and up to his lips before he realized the pair had left her room and were rushing past him down the stairs.

He jammed the cork back into the bottle. He had no need for Dutch courage to face her. He would march straight down those stairs now and tell her . . . tell her . . .

But what could he say? Pardon me, Miss Gratham, but it was *I* who carried you to bed last night? And may I continue to do so for the rest of our lives?

He ran a hand through his hair. Geoff was right; he didn't know how to handle her. Instinct screamed that he forbid her to go anywhere with Geoff, but experience knew he'd never be able to stop her. Changing the woman's answers had always been a good deal easier than changing her mind.

Another pair had tampered with her answers, he now recalled. While plotting to get her alone with Geoff today. The little cabbage-heads no doubt considered compromising their sister a splendid way to bring him up to the mark.

His gaze was drawn out the window to a sky nearly as gray as his mood. On the brooding island in the distance, dense fog shrouded the castle, swirling about it like the serpent of temptation. Caught in a storm, Andrea and Geoff would be stranded. Just the two of them, all night long.

Pushing through the curtains, Richard rushed down-stairs, though he still had no clear idea what he would do. Follow them, surely, but he could hardly plant himself between them in the boat. Not without raising a few too many brows.

One such brow was already raised, he saw as he passed his aunt in the lower hallway. Though admittedly, her smirk was fixed on the bottle of brandy. Thrusting it into her hands, he said not a word as he shoved past.

He found a horse at the stables. Urging it toward the sea, he planned his strategy. He need not be a total boor; there was always a second boat. It was not the trip across he must prevent, after all; only the night ahead.

He could have spared himself the worry, for a verita-ble crowd stood at the jetty. Andrea stood in the center, with Horatio to the right and Geoff to the immediate left. Hovering about were the twins, with their perpetual shadows, Adam and Jamie. Miriam seemed surprisingly jovial, no doubt celebrating the absence of her mama, who through divine mercy and the threatening rain, had opted to remain at the Manor. There was no telling why Elysse chose to brave the weather. She was not doing too well a job of it.

They were all gathered before a single boat, arguing over who must row, with both Horatio and Geoff flexing their masculinity. Clearly uncomfortable, Andrea gave Richard a swift, startled gaze as he dismounted, but before he could become carried away with enthusiasm, she looked abruptly away. *She knows about last night,* he thought, his spirits sinking. *And true to Geoff's prophecy, she hates me.*

Elysse stepped up to anchor herself to his arm. "As it is Richard's boat, let him row," she commanded. "I daresay *he* knows what he is doing."

Richard's suggestion that they use both boats was promptly rejected, for the second craft was missing. Since it seemed the only solution, and it gave him time alone with Andrea, Richard offered to row everyone across in pairs.

By now, it had begun to drizzle. When Elysse demanded to be ferried first, Richard bullied the ever polite Geoff into accompanying her. Horatio went next with Miriam. Not once did the girl try to paw Richard, choosing to make cow eyes at his cousin instead, leading them both to decide she was not half so irritating without her mother.

Richard fought a rising wind as he rowed Adam and Jamie, with each respective twin. The waves, usually tame enough this time of year, slapped at the sides of the tiny craft. It began to rain in earnest. A dripping Andrea, kept waiting on the jetty until last, clearly thought it his intent to punish her. Her spine could not have been stiffer, her glare more unrelenting.

And so, as they moved across the choppy water, he failed to find the adequate words to soothe her. Three times he started to speak, only to shut his mouth in frustration.

The boat barely touched shore before she bounded out of it, showing little more regard for her skirts than she did for his feelings. Richard grumbled as he dragged the craft up to secure it behind a sturdy grouping of rocks.

He turned to the castle, awed as always by the sight looming before him. Inhaling the fresh salty air, he gazed at the circular tower proudly wearing its scars from both battle and the elements. As his father had said, each stone breathed history from every darkened pore. And he was right: Hazard Hall *was* a prize worth fighting for.

His gaze swung to the castle steps, to the damp figure trudging up them, and his brain made the connection. More than this castle was worth the battle. "Andrea, wait," he shouted, running to catch her. "I must speak with you."

She whirled to face him, as angry as the wind

whipping the hair across her face. This had better be worth it, he thought with a sinking heart, for it was clear she meant to give him one devil of a fight.

"Good. I also need to speak to you." Hostility emanated from her in chilling waves. "I have decided I cannot possibly continue with our bargain."

His next few steps were slower. "Why ever not?"

"I cannot trust you; that is why!"

He was about to repeat "Why not?" when Geoff shouted out, "Richard? I say, old man, isn't that your boat drifting out to sea?"

He turned with an oath, thinking he'd failed to secure it after all, but the boat sat where he'd left it. Down the shore to the left, crouched on a rock ledge, Geoff pointed to one bobbing on the water. "Can you reach it?" Richard shouted over the wind, loathe to leave Andrea now. "It would make the return trip simpler."

"I might, if I stand at the end of the rocks."

"Good. I'll be along in a moment."

Lot could not have moored it carefully the last time he used it, Richard thought in exasperation. Just one more thing for which he must be taken to task. Truly, somehow or another, he must convince his aunt the man had to go.

He turned to Andrea, who was once again mounting the steps. "Wait," he blurted out. "Please? Can't you at least tell me what I have done now?"

She halted, letting him climb a few steps closer. Once he reached eye level, she held out an arm to detain him. "You dare pretend innocence?" she attacked. "When we both know you changed my answer last night?"

"I did not!"

"Liar. I cannot be expected to keep my end of our bargain if you can't be trusted to tell me the truth."

Richard strove to control the anger she alone could provoke. "When I swear something, madam, I mean it. Indeed, had I been less scrupulous in keeping my word,

I would not be in this pickle with my aunt, and there would be no need for any bargain. So please, when I say I did not change your answer last night, do me the courtesy of believing it."

She seemed uncertain. It failed to mollify him. "And furthermore, had you been half so scrupulous with *your* word, Mrs. Morton, I'd have no need to change your answer at all."

She looked away, biting her lip. Remembering his own taste of them, Richard's anger began to melt.

She looked up, the blue eyes boring into his. "Tell me, what is your canary doing in my room?"

"I thought you liked the canary," he said, startled.

"I do. But I won't be taken advantage of, do you hear? You mustn't assume our bargain gives you liberty to dump all your unwanted responsibilities on me."

"Unwanted . . . oh, for heaven's sake. I merely feared you might feel odd, waking in a strange room. That you might relish the company."

Though her gaze never left his, the uncertainty had returned. She seemed to soften before him. He climbed a step closer.

"Geoff says he carried me there. Yet it is unlike him to trouble himself so. Did he?"

Richard climbed another step. One alone stood between them. "And if he did not?"

She licked her lips. "Then it must have been you."

This is it, Richard thought breathlessly, moving close to take her hand in his. "Suppose it meant you must wed the one who did. Would you then rather it was Geoff, or me?"

She looked away, clearly as reluctant to face him as to give an answer. He stared into her, willing her to meet his gaze, or better, his lips, but with a strangled *"Geoff!"* she bolted off down the stairs.

He might have winced. He certainly did not bestir himself to follow. Not this time. There was not much sense, for as his aunt had taught, one could not argue with a headstrong woman.

Still, he let himself watch her retreating form. It might be self-inflicted salt in the wound, but he was painfully aware of how little time he had left to watch her at all.

But as always, she caught him off guard. Poising herself on the rocks, she frantically removed her bonnet. Puzzled, he watched her sit to pull off her shoes. *Dear Lord, she couldn't mean to . . .*

He ran, thinking in his own battered state that she melodramatically meant to drown herself, a theory further substantiated as she readied herself to jump. He lunged for her, wrenching her arm as he yanked her to his chest.

"Geoff!" she shouted, fighting to pull away.

"He's not worth this," Richard shouted back, but she continued to shake her head and pull away.

"Geoff!" she repeated, pointing out into the water. "He's drowning!"

CHAPTER
14

Andy stood on the rocks, shouting for help, debating whether or not to jump in after Richard. He had been most emphatic in telling her not to be a bloody fool, to stay on this rock.

But he must be exhausted after all that rowing, she vacillated; he must need help. No matter how he might rage afterward, she could not stand by idly while he drowned.

She frowned at Terese's soggy skirts. No help for it. She sucked in a breath but was spared the folly of jumping as lords Foxley and Bellington thundered past to dive into the waves.

The twins ran close behind. "Don't worry, Andy," they gushed in unison, flinging their arms around her.

"Adam is here," M added.

"Jamie will save Geoff," P exclaimed at the same time.

As their arms dropped abruptly, Andy realized they must be taking their first good look at those waves. Too soon, she was the one providing comfort, assuring them the earl would see to it all four gentlemen emerged from the sea.

And so he did, though it took some time, and Foxley and Bellington were not altogether useless. As both helped Richard drag the too-still Geoff to shore, the twins left Andy to run to their heroes.

"Oh, Adam," said M.

"Oh, Jamie," said P.

"Oh, Richard," Andy longed to say as she approached the spot where he had plopped down on the rocks, looking nearly as lifeless as Geoff.

"We must . . . get him . . . inside," he huffed.

With reluctance, she switched her attention to Geoff. A large welt had formed on his head, but he was breathing, however shallow the process might be. Richard, however, had yet to move, or stop panting. If he didn't soon get out of this driving rain, he would be in a sorrier state than the victim.

But when she turned to ask Foxley and Bellington to help them indoors, she found the two soundly kissing her sisters!

In shock, she barked out her request. Richard glanced up in as much surprise as exhaustion would allow. She smiled unconvincingly, muttering under her breath that it was time she had a serious talk with those two rouges.

Bidding them follow, she climbed the castle steps and pushed through the large oak door at the top. It opened into a huge room, dreadfully cold and virtually empty. Stone walls stretched up into utter black, with large doors yawning into further darkness, hinting of secrets better left undisturbed. Andy shivered, eyeing the mammoth hearth across the room. A fire would be just the thing, she decided.

She crossed over to it. At her instructions, Foxley and Bellington set Geoff on the cold stone floor. "Find some dry coverings," she snapped, shooing the young gentlemen away. "We must make him warm."

As they scurried off, she kneeled beside the patient, who had begun to groan. Poor Geoff. Even if he had so inconveniently interrupted her moment with Richard, he didn't deserve to be in pain. She could make him more comfortable, she supposed. Yanking off his wet boots, as she had so often done for her father, she went to remove his jacket.

"Let me undress him," Richard barked, appearing from nowhere. "There'll be talk enough about this day as it is."

"Are you implying . . . oh, for heaven's sake, I merely tried to make him more comfortable."

He eyed her coldly. "You might better expend the effort on your own behalf. See to a fire. And dry that hair."

Andy realized her lips were trembling. Clamping them shut, she hurried to the far side of the room. Wretched man; he acted as if that moment on the steps had never occurred. Or had she read more into it than had ever been there?

There was no chance to indulge in a useless display of tears, for Elysse was holding court in the corner, making noise enough to raise the dead. The others huddled about her, watching her antics with dismay, the most dejected (and damp) sight Andy had ever seen. Richard thought *she* looked bad? she thought spitefully as she joined them. He should see his precious Elysse. The woman not only looked like a drowning cat, she sounded like one.

One that would soon cause a loss of morale if allowed to continue. "See that pile of loose lumber?" Andy broke in to stop her. "Let's build a fire. And do let's scour the place. We should find something in which to heat water."

"Not in the cellars," Richard bellowed from the hearth. "With all this rain, they're apt to flood. I do not trust the foundations."

"Are you all mad?" Elysse shrieked. "I am not

rummaging through this gloomy relic. I demand to be taken back to the Manor at once."

"We can't possibly move Geoff in this storm."

"Then leave him here. Should I be made to suffer merely because an irresponsible fool fell into the sea? I need to be warm and dry."

"There's no one to row you." Andy, rapidly losing patience, worked to keep her voice low. "Richard certainly cannot. His strength's been tested enough as it is."

"And who are you to make his decisions for him?" Elysse nodded meaningfully in his direction. "Isn't it a trifle premature to be playing lady of the manor? Richard quite detests managing females, you know."

Turning red, for she was quite aware of who Richard detested, Andy nonetheless held her ground. "Let's not bicker, Elysse. As long as we are stranded here, why not make the best of things?"

Her patience received a sneer. Knowing Elysse would never help, Andy turned to the others, who seemed eager to join in. Any action, they seemed to agree, was preferable to listening to Lady Parsett's tirades.

They built their blaze, Miriam surprising them all by proving resourceful with a flint. The way Horatio gushed over this accomplishment, Andy wondered if she might have lost a suitor.

Foxley and Bellington returned with an ancient straw mattress and several dusty sheets. Shaking them out, Andy set herself to making a bed for Geoff. As she did so, Horatio and Miriam emerged from one of those dark doorways with four rusty lanterns and a respectable supply of candles. Miriam, proud of her skill, proceeded to light them at once.

Richard moved Geoff to the mattress, setting himself at the bedside like a guard dog. When Andy tried to resume her nursing, he barked at her to "give the poor man air."

Hurt, she backed away. She grabbed a lamp, deciding that rather than endure his ill humor further, she might as well hunt through the place with the others.

Finding a door with a set of sturdy steps leading down, she looked back at Richard. No doubt it led to the cellars he'd warned them not to explore. In a spurt of defiance, she decided she quite detested managing *males* as well.

But as she descended, she found herself in a narrow enclosure from which room after tiny room seemed to stretch into infinity. Whether it was damper here or just she who was damp, she began to shiver uncontrollably. As a cobweb dragged across her face, she began to think Richard might have been right about those shaky foundations.

All at once, she could not stay here. She spun back toward the stairs, only to bump into a firm, warm chest. To her shame, she screamed.

"Forgive me, Mrs. Morton, please, I had not dreamed you would be startled. Please tell me you are not hurt."

It was Foxley, or Bellington—she could never get them straight—and he seemed endearingly distraught. With a shaky laugh, she shook her head to indicate no real harm had been done. He seemed to fear she might yet faint, for he took the lamp from her hand and set it on the stairs.

"I must speak with you without delay," he began stiffly. "In regards to what transpired between Amanda and myself."

Ah, Foxley! He looked so young and so adorably guilty, she might have relented, had M's future not been at stake. "Good," she told him. "I wish to speak to you as well."

"It happened so suddenly, you see. And Amanda is so . . . so young. So lovely. When she came into my arms today, I could not seem to stop myself. I knew I should, for her sake, but I could not pull away."

"I am in no mood for excuses, my lord."

"Excuses!" he exploded, becoming every bit as haughty as Richard at his worst. "My dear madam, I fully accept that my behavior was *in*excusable. I have come merely to explain why you *must* grant your permission for your sister and I to wed."

"I must? Oh, my."

"I have not made myself clear." He breathed deeply, the boyish features deepening with resolve. "I love Amanda to distraction, Mrs. Morton. I can't imagine life without her."

Oh, my, Andy repeated to herself, stunned into silence.

Taking this for disapproval, Foxley drew in a breath. "I shall agree to any terms you set. Amanda will be distressed if you insist we wait, but I shall see it is done. And you must not trouble yourself over a dowry; your sister is more than treasure enough. She will insist you come live with us, for she can't bear the thought of leaving you, but I have warned you might prefer to stay with Pandora. As much as I hate to admit it, the Bellington estates are a bit grander than my own."

Andy shook her head to clear it. "Stop a moment, please. What is this about P?"

"I say whatever Adam said," piped in Bellington from the top of the stairs. "Do you think we might make it a double affair?"

The twins, married so swiftly? So admirably? "I—I suppose," she said weakly, dropping to sit on a dusty step.

Bellington vanished with a whoop. Foxley stayed long enough to offer to escort her upstairs, but when Andy declined, asking for a moment to catch her breath, he, too, bounded up the stairs. The twins were lucky girls, she thought wistfully.

She was happy for them, truly she was, but with her vow at last fulfilled, with the last of her sisters safely launched, what was left for her to do?

As generous as Foxley's offer might be, she could not live with either twin. She refused to become an object of family charity. Better to earn her way as a seamstress, perhaps. Or even a housekeeper.

She tried not to think of Richard, or of the Season they would no longer need. Oh, she might see him now and again on a rare visit with the twins, but it would never be the same. He'd have a wife by then, and she'd be so dreadfully alone.

I will take the bird, she vowed. If there's to be no Season, I'll make him grant it as part of our bargain.

"Andy," shrieked her sisters, tumbling down the stairs. "You absolutely wonderful person, did you truly say yes?"

As the twins covered her with kisses and hugs, Andy smiled sadly. Heaven help her, she was going to miss these maudlin scenes. The girls, with husbands to look after them, would never again turn to her for help.

"You are not to worry," M assured, seeming suddenly, distressingly mature. "We'd never consider leaving you before Geoff is fully recovered and has time to—*ouch!*"

A confused Andy wondered if P might have pinched her twin's elbow.

"What M means," P corrected, eyes shooting daggers, "is that we will stay at your side as long as you need us."

"What has Geoff to do with anything?" Andy narrowed her gaze considerably. "What scheme have the pair of you been hatching now?"

"Sc-scheme?" stuttered M, blinking her eyes.

"Us?" scoffed P.

"Oh, dear," said Andy with a sigh, seeing too clearly what they'd meant to do. "You've been pushing Geoff at me. Your meddling is what's made him so attentive of late."

"Never say so! Oh, we might have given a nudge, but deep down, Geoff loves you. Indeed, we had great hopes that today he would finally . . . oh, no, Andy, please don't cry."

"She's not crying, M. She's laughing, aren't you?"

She tried to stop, but it was no use. "You're to blame for Horatio, too, I'll wager. Oh, you ridiculous, adorable girls. I came here to see you wed, not the other way round."

"But—but—I thought you loved Geoff?"

"So did I." Andy's smile turned sad. "Once."

P faced her belligerently, hands on her hips. "If not Geoff, then who? We won't rest until we see you happily settled, you know."

"It's him, isn't it?" Speaking softly, taking Andy's hand, M sat beside her on the stairs. "The earl."

There was no need to answer. M seemed to find it right there in her eyes. Jumping up, she grabbed P's arm. "Twin, you and I must see Andy wins this hunt."

"You?"

"Of course us. Don't you dare laugh. Who do you think submitted the correct answer for you last night?"

"As we've had to do for the past several nights," P added. "Heavens, you didn't think Alan Duncan was always the answer, did you? Whoever he is."

Andy felt rather miffed. After all, the cheating had been her idea.

"We won't win anything by sitting down here in the damp." P shivered. "We can as easily put our heads together up beside the fire, you know."

Andy, baffled by the current events, preferred a moment to sit and think. She told her sisters so.

They seemed somewhat dubious. Sensing they were torn by their loyalty to her and a need to be with their young gentlemen, Andy shooed them off. "I'll be along in a moment. You go on, though. Adam and Jamie will be looking for you."

They went, looking back uncertainly a time or two,

but the call of love clearly outweighed any reluctance to leave.

So they'd been changing her answers, Andy thought fondly. Which meant Richard hadn't. Which also meant she was now honor-bound to keep her end of the bargain.

Strange, the direction one's thoughts could take when left with only a lamp for company. Clues flickered through her brain, dancing and stretching like the shadows on the cold stone walls. Ross Duncan, the first Earl of Fairbright, had built this castle to guard the doubloons his queen had granted. Henry Duncan, having been flooded once too often, had moved the entire household to dryer ground. Had he indeed ordered Anson Fyfe to move the contents of the vault? Or was the overseer right in swearing the treasure had never touched his hands? If so, where could it have gone?

Lady Sarah had discouraged her from coming here, Andy recalled again. Richard had likewise tried to keep her from the castle and, failing that, had warned her away from the cellars. As far as she could see, the walls seemed sturdy enough.

Into her mind, brilliant in its clarity, came Alan Duncan's sketch of the vault. Vividly, she saw those dark arrows leading through the narrow enclosures, very like . . .

She held up the lamp, staring straight ahead. Good heavens—could these twisting passageways lead her to the Duncan vault?

She was up in an instant. Which path had been the correct one? The left, surely. She pushed through the cobwebs, choosing one wrong path after another. It was rather like being back in the maze, only without the hedges and without the shovel. Dear me, she thought suddenly. She hoped she would not need to dig.

No wonder Richard had laughed that day. He'd known the real vault was here. Daunted, she wondered if he had thrown in that bit about dangerous foundations as a test. Would she find him waiting at its core again?

She could let that hope die. The man had made it brutally clear there would be no more kisses. She could far better employ her time remembering how to reach the core.

But of course, she realized suddenly—why retrace her entering steps when her most direct route had been in her departure? She need only relive that humiliating retreat and she would soon find herself in the center of this maze.

And so she did, though it proved vastly disappointing. A stout but unlocked door led into a small cubicle— dark, dank, and virtually empty. Shelves lined the dreary walls, holding naught but dust. Bare save for the marble pedestal, this room could not possibly house a small fortune in doubloons.

But inching forward, holding up the lamp, she saw another had been less easily discouraged. The walls beyond the shelves had been hacked into viciously, the indentations into solid stone looking so like the holes in the maze.

Her heart skipped a beat. So someone else thought the treasure might be here, though hopefully he'd found nothing as yet. *Think,* she commanded herself sternly; *try to remember Alan's sketch.* There had been all those dark arrows, the red lettering, and—

An arrow pointing downward! Her heart now began to beat at three times its speed as she dropped to her knees to tap at the flooring. A foolish occupation, she soon realized, for stone does not readily reveal hollow spaces. She rose to look about her. *Think,* she repeated. *Precisely where had that arrow been?*

She went to the marble stand at the center, eyeing it skeptically. One could not hide a fortune in solid marble. But if *it* were hollow . . .

Nothing happened when she tugged at the top, but she

did notice an irregular surface underneath her nails. Closer inspection revealed pins, which she promptly dislodged. To her surprise, and pleasure, the pedestal gave way to fall with unwarranted ease, opening a three-foot gaping hole in the floor.

She reached into it. Paper rustled, but her hands pulled up a metal box. Bringing it up to the light, she half knew what she would find inside. Strange, in her excitement over the doubloons, she had forgotten all about the emerald.

Lady Sarah was right: it *was* a gaudy thing. Still, as she slipped it on her finger, she felt a reluctant awe. The Fairbright emerald. And she had won the right to wear it!

Instantly angry with herself, she wrenched it off. For a nasty moment, it refused to budge—as if it, too, wished to stay there—but that was unforgivably idiotic. Pursing her lips, she dropped it into her reticule before returning to the hole. She had yet to learn what had rustled.

Shining the light inside, she saw the paper at once. Off in the far corner, though, just beyond her grasp, sat a small open chest, gold spilling from its sides to glitter in the lamplight. Bubbling with excitement, she reached for the paper. It was a letter. "To my dear son, Richard," it began.

If you are here, it can only mean that you have set to work restoring our castle. What a lout you must think me, holding you to such a task without providing the means with which to complete it. I could not tell you, that day we spoke, that I'd found the means myself. I must keep it secret from our cousin Reggie, who would waste the lot of it on his gaming.

So I have hidden the doubloons here and bade Aunt Sarah to keep my secret. She has given her word that you are not to be told until you find the treasure yourself. Forgive us for such subterfuge, but we could not risk your cousin learning of it, and preventing you from carrying on the Duncan tradition.

Know that my faith and trust, as well as my love, shall always be with you.

From Duncan father to Duncan son,
Alan Duncan

Dazed, Andy folded the letter so the signature continued to stare up at her. Alan Duncan. That wily dowager; no wonder she hadn't wanted her coming here. Not only had Andy found the emerald and the doubloons, but she had the true answer to today's question. Had she listened to what Lady Sarah fed her, she'd have used Henry as her answer. But he wasn't the last Duncan to touch the treasure; Alan was.

She set the letter in her reticule next to the emerald. She started forward, determined Richard must see it at once, nearly tripping over the hole in her excitement. Remembering the doubloons, she decided it might be wiser to bring him here. Though she should push the pedestal back into place. No sense in alerting anyone else to its whereabouts.

She rushed through the maze and up the stairs, wondering how to convince him to follow her without revealing her secret to the others. She needn't have worried. Horatio and Miriam sat alone in the central hall, ostensibly watching the patient but deeply engrossed in each other. Indeed, Andy had to ask twice where Richard had gone before either noticed she was there.

Shrugging in unison, they remained so infuriatingly unconcerned, Andy wanted to throttle them. "Can you at least tell me which way he went?"

Miriam pointed to the right while Horatio gestured to the left. This threw them into a fit of mutual giggles.

Mrs. Dennison, Andy felt certain, would not enjoy this either. "Tell him to meet me as soon as he can," she told them in exasperation. "In the cellars. In the vault."

She left them still giggling. Anxious now that some-one else might stumble upon Richard's treasure, she rushed down to stand guard over it.

The room was as she had left it, unearthly still and dreadfully dark. To her dismay, the box holding the emerald sat where she'd left it on the floor. Annoyed at her carelessness, she shook her head as she set the box and the lamp on the pedestal.

She began to pace. No longer buoyed by the elation of winning the hunt, she heard every unexpected noise. She found herself wishing Richard would hurry.

Not that she would ever be frightened of some errant mice. It was merely that she was anxious to turn over this ring, she insisted, to have it over and done with. She had two weddings to prepare for, double the trousseaus, and all before Terese returned from Europe to reclaim her clothes.

If only she didn't feel so strong a sense of finality here, of a door slamming firmly in her face.

Where is he? she wondered uneasily, aware now of the sea lapping against the walls. Would the cellars flood? Her flesh began to prickle.

"Richard, is that you?" she whispered. Her voice echoed eerily, bouncing back unanswered. The sense of being watched intensified.

It had to be Richard; no one else knew she was there. Resolute, determined not to be a ninny, she stepped toward the entrance. The presence was palpable now, threatening. "Richard?" she tried again, but a hard, blunt object came crashing down on her head.

She slumped, knees first, to the floor.

Slamming the oak door behind him, Richard stomped over to warm himself at the fire. He noticed with relief

that Elysse was not there. In all, he'd as soon forego the
tantrum, for this one was destined to be a leveler. Lady
Parsett would not enjoy hearing her return trip to the
Manor must be postponed indefinitely. It would be his
fault, he did not doubt, that both boats could now be
counted missing.

The first had drifted off as they rescued Geoff, but the
second could not have done so. Richard had secured it
well beyond the waves. His guess was someone else,
having taken all he could of Elysse's caterwauling, had
been desperate to escape. Not that he could be blamed,
as long as he'd the decency to summon help for the rest
of them.

Horatio would have been the likely culprit, were he
not sitting cozily before the fire. "I say, Richard," his
cousin called out now. "Has Andrea found you?"

Surprised, Richard glanced at the patient, noticing
Andrea wasn't with Geoff. "Looking for me?" he blurted
out, unable to halt the slight stirring of hope.

"Oh, yes," Miriam added. "She seemed most anxious
to find you. Where did she say she'd gone?"

They pointed in opposite directions and giggled like
idiots. "The vault," Geoff croaked. "I say, Richard,
should she be wandering about those cellars?"

Not pausing to answer, nor even consider that his
friend was now conscious, Richard grabbed a lamp and
dashed for the steps. The little idiot. In his mind, he
could see her, prostrate beneath some tumbled stone.

He'd forgotten how dreary it could be in these tunnels.
He hated to think of her going about in the dark and the
damp. It would mean a fever at best. Damned blasted
hunt. If anything happened to her, he'd never forgive his
aunt.

But the world didn't make them more sensible than
Andrea Gratham, he checked himself abruptly. If he
must worry, he should lavish such concern over his own
head. Indeed, he wondered why he hurried after her,

since there was nothing to indicate she sought him for any more than a tongue-lashing. And he'd had more than enough of that from Elysse.

Still, the optimist in him insisted, a good many things could happen when alone with a woman in the dark.

A good many things, but not precisely what he'd hoped. Entering the vault, he found her not waiting to lecture him at all but sprawled in a silent bundle across the hard, cold stone.

CHAPTER

15

"Wake up!"

Something probed into Andy's arm, and she wriggled away from it. Bad enough to be disturbed by all that ungodly screeching, but now Elysse must physically abuse her as well? Merely because the woman wanted to be warm and dry, she could not go about prodding others like some mindless cattle.

Angry now, and prepared to deliver a few choice epithets to this effect, Andy opened her eyes. She might also have popped up, if her head had not throbbed so. She groped for the bedstand, seeking the foul but effective remedy, when she remembered brandy was not to blame. She had fallen. Not here, in this blue bedroom, but in the castle. In the vault.

She turned quickly. It was a foolish move, considering her injured head. She knew who would be attached to the end of that cane. Indeed, the dowager sat there, grinning like the proverbial cat—

Had it been the canary screeching, and not Elysse at all? Taking her head in her hands, fighting disorientation, Andy wondered how the devil she had gotten back in this room.

"Richard carried you," Lady Sarah cackled at her side as if she'd spoken aloud. "Making a naughty habit of it, too."

Andy stared at the cane, longing for the courage to tell her ladyship to go away.

"Now, now, none of that closing your eyes," croaked the dowager, nudging her again. "You've slept more than enough as it is. We have a great deal to accomplish this morning, young lady."

"Oh, Sarah, should you touch her?"

"She's not contagious, Violet," said yet a third voice. "The physician said it is naught but a minor head wound."

"You could show some concern for the poor girl, Amelia. Had I sustained such a blow, I know I'd be prostrate for at least a week."

To Andy's relief, the cane left her to bang on the floor. "Keep quiet, girls, or I shall ask you to leave."

The Tribunal, Andy realized, looking from one to the other. But what could they want with her?

"Sit up and drink your chocolate. Violet, fetch the tray. Amelia can prop up the pillows. Miss Gratham, you and I must talk."

Still somewhat shaken, and annoyed at being fussed over, Andy nearly missed the use of her true name. "Gratham?" she asked, fighting the urge to slink beneath the covers.

"My dear girl, did you think I'd allow you into my nephew's home without having you thoroughly investigated? I once knew your grandfather, you should know. Quite well."

To Andy's astonishment, and growing unease, both ladies Haversham and Makepeace colored profusely.

"*Character,*" the dowager was spouting, punctuating

the words with her cane. "*That's* what Richard needs in a bride."

Andy was left to wonder if her grandfather shared more than a name with her father. Never having known him herself, she was rather daunted by the Tribunal's reaction. Well, if they expected her to grovel in unworthiness before them now, they were doomed to disappointment.

"I will have you know," she told them in her haughtiest tones, "that if his lordship carried me anywhere, it was with neither my knowledge nor consent. Indeed, considering his mood yesterday, I would not have put it past him to have hit me himself."

"Richard?" Lady Makepeace was shocked.

"Lot was the guilty party." The dowager tapped her cane on the floor, dispelling any doubts about her displeasure. "He was caught red-handed with the emerald's box. Though he was no doubt urged on by his accomplice."

Accomplice? Andy shook her head to clear it.

"Richard would hardly have hurt you," Lady Makepeace gushed to her right. "Why, he swam all the way to shore, and then rowed back with his staff to rescue you."

"Thank heavens he first made certain that horrid Lot was locked away. For myself, I could not have slept a wink, had I not known him to be safely behind bars."

"*I* saw to that, Violet," the dowager sniffed. "And I did so for Lot's own protection. Considering Richard's foul mood, he might have murdered him."

"But Lot didn't take the emerald," Andy blurted out, trying to catch up with a world speeding along too rapidly without her. "I have it here."

Scrambling from the bed, she went to the dresser for her reticule. When she dumped its contents onto the bed, though, she found a single damp handkerchief. Perplexed, she glanced up into Lady Sarah's beaming smile.

She has it, Andy realized, feeling the wind leave her lungs. She might have won, fair and square, but the old manipulator had no intention of letting her claim the prize.

Even worse, she had Alan's letter.

Angered beyond belief, Andy drew in a breath to begin her tirade, but the door flew open behind her. Whatever she might have said was lost as the canary began to screech.

Elysse posed on the threshold like the avenging angel. Or perhaps more a demon, for her eyes glittered with a most unholy triumph. A glow met, and perhaps surpassed, by the emerald sparkling on her outstretched hand.

"How delighted I am to see you all assembled here," Elysse gloated, ignoring the bird. "What do you think, Andrea darling? Doesn't this gem look divine on my hand?"

Andy, who had gone to the cage to quiet the bird, could not speak. The sense of betrayal stung too deep. Miriam Dennison was one thing, but for Lady Sarah to give the ring to such a blatant fortune-hunter?

"Dear Aunt Sarah," Elysse gushed, sickeningly sweet as she approached them. "I imagine you'll be leaving for London soon? It will be so uncomfortable for you here, after all, once Fairbright has its new countess."

"Never said you weren't a clever chit." All but purring, the dowager held out her hand. "Still, it is for Richard to place it on the winner's finger. If you please?"

With a smirk for Andy's benefit, Elysse removed the ring and set it in the outstretched hand.

"Thank you. Now, if you please, I suggest you pack your things and leave. And do make haste. Should you dally, I might be tempted to place you in jail with your confederate."

"I beg your pardon?"

"Your partner in crime. That cursed Lot. I have

watched you from the start, Lady Parsett. You were never the one I wanted for Richard, even without your skullduggery."

Though both Andy and Elysse stood with their jaws open, the latter recovered first. "Do you truly think it's your choice to make, Sarah? I've won your absurd hunt, and you've no choice but to acknowledge it publicly. You gave your word, remember." Elysse grabbed for the ring. "The word of a Fairbright."

"So I did." The dowager kept the ring tightly clasped in her hand. "But had you read the rules, as instructed, you would do better than to come sniveling to me now."

"I am not sniveling. I followed your wretched rules."

A white eyebrow raised. "Oh? You answered yesterday's question correctly, then?"

What was the dowager driving toward now? Andy wondered. One of those underlying motives Richard complained about?

"Of course I did. Everyone knows Henry Duncan was the last to touch that treasure. You told me so yourself."

"And you trusted the memory of an aging woman? Foolish child; you've disqualified yourself. So even had you come by this ring honestly, you could not win, and I cannot with any clear conscience allow you to remain."

The dowager hadn't *given* Elysse the ring? Of course not; Elysse had *stolen* it. *That* was why the canary had screeched so desperately last night.

Elysse had turned nearly as purple as Lady Haversham's gown. "You old witch! You tricked me!"

"Yes, and I did so enjoy doing it." Lady Sarah rested both hands on her cane, smile stretching from ear to ear. "Now, what is it to be? A carriage, or the jail cart? Poor Lot would adore companionship in that cell."

"Jail? You're bluffing; you cannot prove a thing."

"Perhaps not. That would be Richard's task, of course."

"Richard?" With a slow, spreading smile, Elysse

glided to the door. "Yes, do let's have Richard decide. There are ways of circumventing your silly rules, Sarah. Just wait and see." With a flounce of her skirts, Elysse was out the door and slamming it behind her.

Andy, who'd been warming with hope, now felt chilled. Circumventions? In all the excitement, she'd forgotten about her own bargain with Richard.

It was so quiet in the room that when Lady Haversham began tearing a slip of paper, Andy jumped.

"I did warn you not to wager on her, Violet," Lady Makepeace tittered, smugly waving her own slip.

"Oh? And do you truly suppose Miriam Dennison was clever enough to answer the question either?"

"Do stop bickering, girls. If you must know, only one entrant was clever enough."

"We have a winner? But who?"

Supporting herself with her cane, the dowager hobbled toward Andy. "One who knew our Richard well," she said with a gentle smile as she beckoned Andy to a corner of the room. "Only one who did could know where to find the answer."

"But I can't take the ring." Horrified, Andy shook her head. Honor-bound as she was to refuse him, Richard would only end up in Lady Parsett's clutches, after all. Better he marry Miriam Dennison. "I don't deserve it, either."

"Stop fiddling with that bird, girl, and come here."

It was an order, Andy recognized, and she dared not disobey it.

Turning her back to her friends, Lady Sarah placed a folded paper in her hands. For a confused moment, Andy thought it to be the day's question, again overlooked on the floor, until she belatedly recalled the hunt was done.

"In her greed, Lady Parsett overlooked the real treasure," the dowager whispered. "This letter, as you no doubt guessed, was the true objective of my hunt."

"You've been prodding me," a dazed Andy hissed

back. "Just as the vicar told me you do to your nephew. By telling me not to go to the castle, you knew full well I'd be all the more determined to go there."

"Forgive me, but I needed your help. I'd begun to fear Richard would never find those doubloons. You can't know how many times I regretted that promise. But sadly enough, I understood Alan's need for secrecy. One hates to speak ill of the dead, particularly one's own son, but Reggie could be a proper scoundrel. Richard was always worth two of him."

"You old fraud," Andy was startled into saying, "you love him as much as I."

The dowager chuckled at her unwitting admission. "I took the liberty of placing Alan's letter in the enameled box as your answer. Violet and Amelia are proper sticklers when it comes to our wagers, and showing them this letter was the only way you could have won."

"But I don't understand. You wanted me to win?"

"I *expected* you to. Character, my child, always wins out." The dowager smiled at her sadly. "I should have married Gerry. I have oft regretted that I did not. He was a wild youth, yes, but he outgrew it. Had I patience . . ."

Inhaling deeply, she raised her head high. "But then I would never have known what it meant to be a Fairbright. And my nephew would not now be waiting in his study for you."

Erupting in a chorus of "Sarah, no!" ladies Makepeace and Haversham both ripped their wagers to bits.

Lady Sarah gave Andy's arm a squeeze. "Hurry and dress, child. Richard awaits you."

In a fever of anxiety, Richard paced across the room. Confound his aunt for not telling him who had won. And double-confound her for banning him from Andrea's room.

Picturing her as she had been last night, so limp and lifeless, he felt the same impotent rage. He should have been at her side, protecting her, not chasing off after some silly boat Lot had already stolen. For that matter, he should be at her side now. Who was his aunt to stop him?

He went for the door, prepared to storm the Bastille, but a smiling Elysse stood in his way. She was as beautiful as ever, but he saw none of this as she pushed past into the room.

He stared, slowly assimilating what her appearance could mean. He felt the noose tightening around his neck.

"Darling, you cannot imagine the dreadful things your aunt just said to me."

"Of course I can," he snapped. "I've lived with the woman for twenty-five years."

Her eyes went hard; even she saw the current futility in tears. "In that case, isn't it time you break free of her leading strings? Tell her you want nothing more to do with her hunt!"

"What, and go back on my word?"

Her entire face stiffened. "I hesitate to say this, but that awful woman offers no alternative. You must choose, Richard. It's either her or me."

He did not bother to scoff at her ultimatum, for he'd begun to realize what he should have noticed at once. If Elysse had the emerald, she would be flashing it in his face. "You don't have the ring?" he blurted out.

"Does it matter? Darling, don't you see? If we bend to her rules now, she'll make our lives miserable forever."

"Do you have the ring?"

She stomped her foot. "I had it, you ridiculous man. Your aunt took it away from me."

As she ranted on about the dowager's chicanery, Richard sighed in relief. The old manipulator. He should have known she would never let Elysse win. "I'm sorry," he lied when the woman wound down, "but there is nothing I can do."

"Don't you mean there is nothing you *will* do?"

He shrugged. She slapped him, good and hard. "Cad, I wasted my youth on you. You owe me more than this."

He could have told her he was the one who'd lavished his time and emotion, but he simply didn't care to waste another second. "If you are finished," he said coldly instead, "I'm expecting someone else."

"Who? That Gratham chit? Don't flatter yourself. Were he to ask, she'd go off with Geoff in a shot."

Fighting the urge to return her slap, Richard grabbed her arm to escort her to the door.

"You mean to have her, don't you?" Eyes gleaming, she seemed quite ugly in her spite. "Bloody fool. You believed that Little-Miss-Innocence act? All she sought was the ring, you know. She and Lot worked together to steal it from you."

Richard hesitated, his distrust of women fueling his uncertainty. Andrea had lied at the start; could she have been lying all along?

The doubt dissolved as swiftly as it had come. If he'd learned to be cynical about women, Elysse was the one to teach him. And she was far too pleased with herself now.

"I see," he began. "In any case, we shall soon have the truth. Once Lot learns of the jail term he faces, I daresay he'll be only too quick to give the name of his accomplice."

She paled. "Accomplice?"

"Of course. He was hardly clever enough to manage on his own."

"You can't mean me? Why, I . . . I merely told him to follow her. I am not to blame if he became exuberant."

He flung her away before he could throttle her. "Is there no end to your greed? She could have been killed by that blow. You could be facing a murder charge, and for what? A bloody stone?"

"You don't understand." She tugged at his sleeve, beseeching him. "I was at my wits' end. I am being dunned by every creditor in London, Richard. Please, remember what we once meant to each other. Do not turn me away."

He could not bear to look at her. "I can do nothing for you, Elysse. This is a matter for the local magistrate."

"Pompous fool!" With a sniff, Elysse showed her true colors. "I have little to fear. You can do nothing without proof. After all, who would take the word of that petty criminal against a lady?"

Sadly enough, she was right. In utter disgust, he yanked free of her grasp. "Whatever happens, Lady Parsett, you have overstayed your welcome here. I want you packed and out of my house within the hour."

"You should have taken me, Richard. God knows who your aunt will force upon you."

"I know my aunt's choice, madam," he bellowed. "Do you honestly think me so manipulated?"

"I suggest you lower your voice, then," she hissed, "or you'll soon have that Dennison dowd descending upon you."

He lowered his voice to a deadly calm. "I'd as soon take my chances. Quite frankly, I'd wed a snake before I'd choose you for my wife."

She held her head high—he had to grant her that—as she marched from the room. Indeed, she retained so much pride that without his smarting cheek to prove otherwise, he might wonder if he had somehow proposed to her.

He was shaking his head, still recoiling from the nastiness of that scene, when a firm knock sounded on the door. If that is Miriam Dennison, he thought in disgust, I think I shall spit.

He went behind his desk before calling out for his visitor to enter.

Framed in the doorway, Andrea tried a tentative smile. Her hand trembled as it held out the emerald.

Richard felt a relief, so profound, it was all he could do not to kiss her. He should have known she would never let him down. That she would risk hell and high water to keep her end of the bargain.

"Forgive me, my lord. I hope I am not disturbing you."

He followed her gaze to the hall, realizing she must mean Elysse. "No, that matter is quite settled."

"I see." Her voice seemed flat, more the tone of a condemned criminal than a happy bride-to-be. "Perhaps I should leave."

"No, do come in and make yourself comfortable. I trust you are feeling more the thing?"

She sat in his favorite chair, imprinting her form and scent into its cushions. No one else, he decided fatuously, must ever sit in it again.

"I am fine. I can only hope poor Geoff fares as well."

Geoff, always Geoff. Feeling as if he'd been doused with ice water, Richard lowered himself into his chair. "He's well enough. From what I hear, he's already up and shouting for his breakfast."

He'd meant to be witty, but resentment got the best of the remark. Then again, this was no time for humor. There was this nagging little business to get through first.

"I imagine you know why I am here."

She could have been facing a firing squad. Discouraged, Richard wondered why he persisted. "I do. Will you do me the honor of becoming my wife, Miss Gratham?"

"No."

He felt himself flinch. Really, what had he expected? They both knew Geoff waited upstairs.

Sighing, she placed the emerald on the desk between them, sliding a piece of paper underneath. A note? he wondered bitterly. A let-us-remain-friends missive that truly meant farewell? He refused to look at it.

"As long as that is settled," she said with an abrupt sigh, "I have one last request. Instead of your help with the twins, do you think I might have your canary?"

"You'd sacrifice your sisters' Season for a bird?"

She looked at her hands. "Their Season is no longer necessary. It appears the twins will be wed to your friends before the year is out."

Damn Adam and Jamie for their impatience. And double-damn his own blindness. Had he been as quick to see what he wanted, had he gone after Andrea as single-mindedly, Richard too could be making wedding plans. That first time on the hill, he should have taken her in his arms and kissed her silly, but instead, he had gone full steam ahead, doing and saying every wrong thing.

"Take the damned bird, then," he snapped. "Take Geoff as well."

"I . . . well, yes . . . I suppose I should." She hurried to the door, leaving nothing behind but her imprint in his favorite chair.

Tensing, he watched her pause, nodding toward his desk. Ah, the note, he thought bitterly. He had wondered when she would get around to it.

"I, uh, that is for you. I meant to bring it to you at once, but I . . . well, you have it now. I hope it will make all the difference in your life, my lord. I wish . . . I hope you might have a happy one."

"Go to Geoff," he told her flatly, staring out the window at the hill.

She ran then, as if her feet could not take her fast enough. Left alone in his study, Richard could not bear the sudden silence. The emptiness.

He did not so much as glance at the letter as he stormed from the room.

CHAPTER
16

Will I never learn? Andy wondered as she jammed her belongings into the portmanteau. She'd heard Richard just now as he raged against his aunt. Somehow he'd learned, no doubt through Elysse, that the dowager had wanted her former love's granddaughter for his bride, and he understandably wanted no part of it. She'd seen Elysse's gloating sneer. Only an imbecile would continue to hope that reading his father's letter would make any difference at all.

If he felt anything, it was impersonal gratitude, and perhaps relief, that Andy had refused him. He would not come to her. There would be no arguments, no begging her to stay.

Yet at the knock, she nonetheless looked up hopefully.

"We can't do it," P pronounced, bursting into the room to fling herself, face first, on the bed. "It isn't fair."

Behind her, M entered the room nodding, her lower lip trembling. "I mean to tell Adam this instant," she said, likewise plopping down. "I can't possibly marry him now."

It was one thing when they thought Andy would marry Geoff, or even the earl, but leave her alone? They'd rather die old maids on the highest shelf, they sobbed, than leave their dear, sweet sister to such a lonely fate.

Joining them on the bed, she tried to tell them not to be such ninnyhammers, that she would be quite happy on her own, but perhaps the tears were contagious. Sniffing freely, she found herself telling them all, from Lady Sarah's confession to Richard's abrupt dismissal. She was surprised at how nice it felt, being comforted for a change.

They might have remained there indefinitely, indulging in the most disgusting orgy of tears, had Geoff not come to the door.

"What a batch of waterspouts," he teased, remarkably robust and cheerful. "Must have swallowed too much rain. I say, girls, could you take your tears elsewhere? I have something I must discuss with your sister."

The girls brightened considerably as they scrambled to their feet. Glancing from her to Geoff in a most appraising way, they scampered from the room.

"May I come in?" Geoff asked from the doorway.

"I—I don't think that would be proper," she stammered, jumping up to join him instead.

"Proper? My dear girl, when I am about to become one of the family? I know I've been somewhat remiss in saying this, Andy-girl, but I do think it is time you and I thought about our future. What say we get shackled?"

It was too much, of course, so she began to cry again.

"I say, what is this? Richard said you'd be delighted."

He stood there, arms raising and falling helplessly, as if he hadn't the least idea what to do. "I say, if your distress stems from that business years back—"

"It has nothing to do with the past; it's the future." Poor Geoff; how could she make him understand? "Can you honestly imagine spending the rest of our lives together?"

"There are worse things, I would think. Drat that Richard; he said you'd fly to me with open arms."

"I daresay he did."

"Well, I like that. I am proposing to you, silly chit; you should not be crying."

"Oh, Geoff, I'm sorry, but you must see we'd never suit. I'd bully you dreadfully. Being as nice as you are, you'd allow it. And we would both hate that no end."

"Not I. Never."

Sheer bluster. She could see he half agreed with her. And she could half see his relief. "I love you as a brother, Geoff," she told him gently. "I could never be your wife. Not when I love—" She broke off, unable to go on.

"So that is the way of it." He sighed heavily. "Double-drat that Richard."

"Yes, well . . ." Firmly wiping her eyes, she looked back at the portmanteau. "His lordship has made it quite clear that we've overstayed our welcome. I don't suppose we could borrow your carriage for our return to London?"

"Of course. I hope you don't mind if I don't accompany you?"

Andy, belatedly remembering his recent injury, felt instantly contrite. "Oh, Geoff, I'd forgotten how your head must hurt."

"Not my head, Andy-girl," he said softly. "More like my heart."

Touching her gently on the chin, he smiled sadly and left the room.

Outside the door, the twins exchanged a worried glance.

Dressed in his buckskins, Richard had decided to get through the day by working himself to exhaustion. He was on his way to the stables to fetch a horse when he heard a timid "My lord?" behind him. He whirled to find one of the younger Miss Grathams nervously twisting her hands. Where was the other? he wondered, knowing they always traveled in pairs.

She swallowed. "I know you are fearfully busy, and I do hate to disturb you, but I fear for my sister, my lord. She went up that hill hours ago, the one overlooking the Manor, but she has yet to return."

Given that it was the livelier of the two, Richard had little doubt that the missing twin was deep into mischief. "Be patient," he told her sister. "I daresay we shall hear from her shortly."

He turned to leave, but she persisted. "She was distraught, you must realize. I very much fear what she might . . . what might have become of her."

"Really, Miss Gratham, I can't see what you mean me to do."

"I thought you might talk to her. Sh-she respects you a great deal. If you were to tell her it doesn't matter about Geoff, that she was right to refuse his offer, and that many more offers will come her way, I think she might not feel quite so, er, desperate then."

Completely baffled by now, Richard took the girl by the arms, fighting the urge to shake her. "What has Geoff to do with your twin?"

"P? Why, nothing. I'm talking about Andy, of course."

With a broad smile, P watched her sister's performance. How brave of M to overcome her fear of the earl. But as P explained, someone had to coax him up that hill while she bullied Andy in the same direction. The pair needed one more chance alone together, she and M had agreed. And they must do whatever they could to manufacture it.

She wished she could be there to see Andy's face when, instead of a distraught Geoff, Fairbright himself came riding up to her. Dear, kind-hearted Andy, who could forget her own heartbreak to comfort Geoff in his, deserved this time alone with her earl. Indeed, P thought, if she and M had anything to say about it, Andy would have a lifetime with him.

And from way the earl had gone dashing off, the future looked bright indeed. Stepping forward to congratulate M, P mentally began making wedding plans. Andy's, and her own.

Behind her, Lady Sarah grinned in the doorway.

A hundred demons plagued his heels as Richard raced along the road to the hill. Why had she refused Geoff? And why was she now so dejected, she would climb to the hill where they'd first met and—

Do what? Heaven help him, his emotions had been so lacerated, he wasn't thinking clearly at all. The woman could hardly take her life on so gentle a slope.

Halting the horse and slowly dismounting, he proceeded into the copse at a more cautious pace. Even given a more respectable cliff, Andrea would scorn such a melodramatic gesture. The twins were plotting again, he should have realized. If he could but clear his brain, he would know in an instant what the young she-devils had in mind.

But as he neared the clearing, all hope of clarity left him, for he found Andrea standing there placidly, if a trifle sadly, looking out over the estate. She wore her dull, dusty traveling clothes, looking so like a governess, or someone's maiden aunt, that Richard felt himself drift back in time.

She whirled to face him, just as she'd done that first time, and he felt his world spin with her. Sometimes in life a man is granted a second chance, he thought with a surge of hope. God help him, this time he must do it right.

"Forgive me," he said, approaching slowly. "I had no idea anyone else would be here."

She stared at him, silently pleading with those eyes. *Her lashes are damp*, he thought with dismay. *Andrea crying?*

"Please forgive the intrusion," he said softly, hoping to coax a smile. "But I am incurably inquisitive. I needed a peek at Fairbright Manor, you see."

She tilted her head, the tiniest of grins forming on those full, red lips.

"I beg your indulgence for disrupting your solitude, Miss Gratham, but—"

"Andy," she corrected, the grin widening. "Just call me Andy."

"Actually, I'd hoped to call you Lady Fairbright."

Something leapt into her eyes, something that set his pulse racing. "But I thought Elysse—"

"Lady Parsett is gone," he said firmly, pointing to the carriage leaving the drive.

"Oh. I'm sorry. I hope it was nothing I said or did."

She stood stiffly, hands clasped so firmly her knuckles gleamed white. Watching, Richard began to understand. All this time, she'd thought he wanted Elysse. Could he have been as wrong about Geoff?

"I asked Elysse to leave," he explained, watching every nuance of her face, "but I'd rather hoped you would stay."

"Me?"

"This has nothing to do with the hunt, or our bargain, Andrea. I am asking you to marry me, for myself. Given my present financial status, I'm not precisely the catch of the Season, but I do love you with all my heart."

"Oh . . . oh, Richard." And bursting into a fresh set of tears, she fell into his arms.

Gently removing her bonnet, he slid his hands into her hair, displacing hairpins as he brought her face to his. So sweet, he thought, tenderly touching her lips with his own.

She responded eagerly. As the kiss deepened, he

ignored the whys and hows, yielding instead to the utter
wonder of the moment. Andrea was here, and, somehow, she was his.

"Have you any idea how much I adore you, Miss
Just-call-me-Andy?" he said when he could finally bear
to pull his lips away.

Her smile was more than he'd ever dared hoped for.
"Not quite yet, my lord, but I'm eager to learn."

Whereupon he had no choice but to kiss her again.

Lady Sarah entered her nephew's study to find the
Gratham twins watching Richard and his future bride
descend the hill. Their sighs of satisfaction could be
heard at the other end of the house.

"Don't be so smug," she snapped, chuckling as they
both jumped. "They've a great deal of sorting out to do
yet. Both the ring and his father's letter lie untouched
here on his desk."

"Andy will see he reads that letter," the livelier one
boasted with a toss of her curls. "Just like she found his
fortune for him."

"And his lordship shall see she gets the ring." Though
speaking more softly, the other was no less determined.
"That's what you wanted, isn't it?"

The dowager clucked. "Little cheats; you've been
listening in keyholes. You should be ashamed of yourselves."

Wagging a finger, the lively one looked her straight in
the eye. "No more than yourself. Though I daresay we
should all have worked together, Lady Sarah. We would
have brought them together much sooner that way."

The dowager raised a haughty brow, prepared to give
the chit the setdown she deserved, only to realize the girl
had a point. Weren't half as silly as they first appeared,
these two.

"Oh, look, P," the other one sighed. "Don't they look
deliriously happy? Doesn't it make you happy too?"

The one called P smiled, just as fatuously, to which the dowager gave a grunt. "And has it not yet occurred to the pair of you that with things settled so admirably, life will seem rather tame in the future? That there shall be no further need for your schemes?"

The pair looked at each other, and then turned back to her with a grin. "We shall just have to see about that," they said in unison. "Won't we?"

The dowager raised a brow again, this time in contemplation. The pair showed great promise, far more than Amelia or Violet. Not that she meant to abandon old friends, but the staid and predictable London Season, not to mention her nephew and his new wife, could always use another Tribunal.

Yes, indeed, they would just have to see about that.